THE RECIPIENT

Barry Ahlsten

Schuler Books

www.TheRecipient.com

Chapbook Press

Schuler Books
2660 28th Street SE
Grand Rapids, MI 49512
(616) 942-7330
www.schulerbooks.com

The Recipient

ISBN 13: 9781948237215

Library of Congress Control Number: 2019937270

Printed in the United States by Chapbook Press.

Table of contents

Acknowledgement

To those who know there is more...

To those who want to see behind the curtain...

To those who are not afraid of passion...

Welcome to the world of

THE RECIPIENT

Every good and perfect gift comes from above,
coming down from the father of lights...

The Players

BIO:

Name:	Bear McQuade
Category:	Human male
Status:	Righteous, chosen
Mission:	(Long term) Find recipient; stay alive
Current Assignment:	Unaware of his assignment regarding the portal
Strengths:	Heart; seer
Weaknesses:	Overly cautious; Unable to overcome his past
Knowledge of eternal law:	Intermediate
Notes:	In the opinion of this overseer, the subject is not ready for activation

The wild card

BIO:

Name:	Reece Bernell
Category:	Human male
Status:	Reprobate, hostile
Mission:	Classified
Current Assignment:	Under enemy manipulation regarding the portal
Strengths:	Extremely determined, focused
Weaknesses:	Seared conscience
Knowledge of eternal law:	Minimal

The Crime Boss

BIO:

Name:	Jennifer Bernell
Category:	Human female
Status:	Conflicted; seeking; non-hostile
Mission:	Subject is unaware of her mission
Current Assignment:	Unaware of her involvement in the portal project and must remain so
Strengths:	Capable of self-sacrifice
Weaknesses:	Easily distracted; vain
Knowledge of eternal law:	Minimal

Notes: Mother of Missy

The trophy wife

BIO:

Name: Missy

Category: Juvenile human female

Status: Innocent, vulnerable

Mission: Classified

Strengths: Violin prodigy; anointed;
                    forerunner potential

Weaknesses: Missing father influence

Notes: Unusual access through
                    dreams. **She must be
                    protected at all costs.**

The Prodigy

BIO:

Name: Zavan

Category: Celestial

Status: Righteous

Mission: Protect Bear McQuade; assist
                                him in his quest to find the
                                recipient

Current Assignment: Classified project involving the
                                portal

Strengths: Passion; risk-taker

Weaknesses: Passion; risk-taker

Knowledge of

eternal law: Expert level

Notes: Can get too emotionally
                                invested in his mission

The Guardian

BIO:

Name:	Dagon
Category:	Celestial
Status:	Extremely hostile
Mission:	Maintain/grow current territory
Current Assignment:	Find out who has been called to open portal; destroy same
Strengths:	Brilliant; Patient; Advanced knowledge of spiritual warfare tactics
Weaknesses:	Overconfidence
Knowledge of eternal law:	Expert level
Notes:	Very dangerous; has developed an extensive network

The Fallen

BIO:

Name:	Neal
Category:	human male
Status:	Conflicted; wounded; agnostic
Strengths:	Intelligence, loyalty, knowledge of legal system; good at reading people
Weaknesses:	Cannot define himself outside of his past
Knowledge of eternal law:	Virtually non-existent
Notes:	Subject has a sense he is in Bear's life for a reason; cannot explain it

The Mystery Man

The Recipient

Chapter one

Shamayim

On a bluff overlooking the valley stood a lone figure with intense blue eyes gazing at the sheer cliffs far away on the other side. He had been here so many times he had lost count, but it never got old. A familiar sense of awe and serenity swept over him as he took it all in.

"Zavan." Hearing his name snapped him out of his reverie. He looked back to see his old friend Dagon. "It's time." Said Dagon as he also looked out over the valley. "This is the perfect place to practice." The two friends were interrupted by the sound of a commotion. As the rumbling got closer, the ground began to shake, and a great army came into view. The two saw soldiers without number; some were on horses, others rode giant eagles, while the rest marched on foot. An almost blinding golden light emanated from their armor.

"We better fall in", Dagon said, "or we'll miss the action".

They found their positions and marched along with their fellow soldiers, listening for the order. When they heard it, they immediately split into two groups, with each regiment flying its own flag. They picked up speed and practically flew over the terrain. When they were in place, they all came to attention: two great armies, facing each other. No one moved a muscle. They were all waiting for the signal.

The Recipient

They had practiced this maneuver so any times, Zavan knew every move, every step by heart. The question came to his mind again, but he refused to allow the words to be formed. The trumpet sounded a long blast, signaling the attack. Immediately, the front lines of both armies launched themselves forward toward the center. As they met, the sounds of clashing metal echoed through the valley. At the next trumpet blast, Zavan and Dagon sprinted toward the battle line and engaged the 'enemy'. The two had been practicing; they fought back to back with precision movements that looked like a perfectly choreographed dance. Three short blasts from the trumpet signaled the end of battle practice. Zavan looked around and saw smiling faces, soldiers helping each other up from the ground, and no blood anywhere. It was impossible to get hurt while practicing in Shamayim.

"See you there?" Dagon casually asked Zavan. It was their custom to ride their horses up the lookout point on Mount Terazim after practice. "Wouldn't miss it!" Zavan replied.

The trip up the mountain went quickly, and they got to their favorite spot and sat down in the grass. It was the highest peak in the area, and the atmosphere was so clear they could see for hundreds of miles in every direction. The view encompassed prairies surrounded by giant evergreen and cedar forests, and the river winding its way through the jungle on the east side. "I never get tired of this. I almost wonder if it's too good to be true. Or if it will last." Zavan said, almost mesmerized by the beauty of the place. "Why-" Dagon

began to ask, when Zavan cut him off – "Don't".
Undaunted, Dagon continued, "Why are we practicing
for battle? We have no enemies. I know you've been
asking yourself that question. Everyone has." Zavan
replied, "I don't want to think about that." Dagon kept
going, "Does it make you wonder if there's something
the creator isn't telling us?" Zavan looked thoughtfully
at the expanse before him for a few seconds and said,
"How could someone who made all this... this perfect
world... this peace, this..." Zavan struggled for the right
words. "How could we not trust him?"

A large crowd was gathered at the Amphitheater in
Mezzano Park. The huge ivory colored clamshell-like
structure made for perfect acoustics. There were
thousands seated, waiting to see, waiting to hear what
was coming. Everyone was talking about it. As the
curtain was raised, silence fell over the whole group.
The figure onstage appeared with his back to the
audience; they could see his broad shoulders with a
purple velvet cape over them that reached the ground,
and his jet-black hair cascading halfway down his back.
The figure slowly turned around and revealed his
identity. It was Lucifer. He knew how to make an
entrance. It seemed, though, that there was something
different about him. The gemstones embedded in his
neck and upper chest pulsated with light. He made no
apologies that he was the most glorious celestial being
ever created. Unlike before, he reveled in his beauty.
For the first time, he was deliberately drawing attention

to himself. He watched the crowd watching him. He lifted his arms up in front of himself, palms up, took a deep breath, and opened his mouth wide. The sound that came out was breathtaking. There was not only a melody coming from him, but the sound of harmony, percussion... an entire orchestra. Everyone was transfixed on him. When he began to sing the words of the song, most of the crowd became enraptured. It was magical. The enchanting nature of the music masked the fact that the message was unfamiliar. Up until that moment, all songs had been about the creation or the creator. In the back row Dagon sat and watched, very much enthralled by what he was seeing and hearing.

Lucifer did not use words like rebellion or subversion, but he had begun a campaign - he was planting seeds. He would do many, many concerts, spontaneous oratories, discussions and other events designed to captivate as many as possible. He subtly raised doubts about the creator's motives, never railing against him, but rather speaking of him in glowing terms, yet leaving lingering doubts. His speeches almost took a patronizing tone, as if Lucifer was trying to save the creator from himself.

Zavan was riding his horse at the base of the city wall, admiring its intricate stonework and the jewels that were embedded in layers, which shone brilliantly in multiple colors. The colors that emanated from the jewels created a mist that hung in the atmosphere.

The Recipient

Zavan ran his hands through the color, and watched it seep through his fingertips. The haze went all the way to the top of the wall, higher than twenty horses. "The color almost seems to get more intense every time you look at it." Zavan instantly recognized the voice of Kiandra, his mentor. He turned around to see her also immersed in the beauty of the wall. Kiandra was a head shorter than Zavan, had waist length brown hair, big green eyes, and had the appearance of agelessness. Zavan was amazed by her wisdom, and that she would so freely share it with him.

"Lucifer." Zavan said. Instantly a serious look came over Kiandra's face. "I've been watching him and his... actions. What is he up to?" Zavan demanded. "Does the creator know?" Kiandra replied, "Nothing escapes his watchful eye." Zavan queried, "Why isn't he doing anything?" "We aren't meant to know some things." Kiandra said, wishing it weren't true. "I sense something coming from Lucifer that I can't describe. It just doesn't feel right... and I sense it's spreading." Zavan responded, "I'm concerned about Dagon. He's been spending a lot of time listening to Lucifer." Kiandra stroked Zavan's horse under its neck while she thought, then said, "Maybe you should check on him."

Zavan went through the main gate into the city, which was divided into four quadrants. It was designed with aesthetics as the primary focus, as all the cities were – in the center was a park with a ring of immaculately manicured trees surrounding a beautiful bronze fountain that had twelve dolphin sculptures in a circle, shooting water out of their mouths toward the center.

The Recipient

This city was created using only gothic architecture; there were towering spires and dramatic flying buttresses everywhere. Zavan went to the main library and walked up the marble stairs to the massive double doors, deep in thought. He entered the lobby, passing under a huge chandelier. He made his way up several wide marble staircases and then to the archives room in the east wing. He spotted Dagon in a study nook and approached him. Dagon had several ancient-looking books open on the table and was lost in thought. "Still studying eternal law?" asked Zavan. Dagon's head jerked up with a start. "Zavan." He said. "Didn't hear you come in." "You've been preoccupied lately." Zavan said, not wanting to waste time with pleasantries. Dagon said, "I've been reevaluating a great many things." Then they both said at the same time, "Lucifer…" There was silence for a moment as they searched each other's faces. Zavan went first, "This concerns me." "Not to worry, my friend. Lucifer is the most brilliant archangel in existence. He sees things so clearly -" Zavan interrupted, "But his ambitions… recently he has even spoken of being equal to the creator!" Dagon's face hardened, and for the first time Zavan felt a barrier creep in between him and his friend. "You seem far away from me, Dagon. I don't understand." Dagon said something that surprised Zavan as well as himself: "No one, not even you, will keep me from my destiny."

As Zavan walked down the steps of the library, he struggled with a feeling he had never known. He noticed that Lucifer's messages were beginning to take

a more urgent tone. Shamayim was being infected...
divided.

Zavan waited outside the boardroom where Kiandra
was in a high-level meeting with twelve others of her
rank. As they filed out of the room, she noticed Zavan
pacing, looking very troubled. He noticed that everyone
coming out of the room also looked grim. As their eyes
met, Zavan knew instinctively that whatever was
happening was monumental, and it was not good.
Kiandra said, "Walk with me." As they walked outside
through a grove of olive trees, some of Zavan's peace
returned. Kiandra told him, "We believe that Lucifer is
planning something big. There is a rumor he intends to
make his move when the three moons align." The
heavenly bodies had been created for signs as well as
marking times and seasons. Since their moons only
lined up once every seven generations, Zavan quickly
connected the dots – Lucifer was using the timing to his
advantage. Zavan responded, "Very strategic. He's
leveraging our understanding of the creation in order to
influence us. He's taking every advantage he can get."

Some time later, Zavan was in a grove of giant mango
trees, enjoying the sweet, delicious fruit, when he heard
the sound of a horse's hooves pounding the ground at
full speed. He ran to the edge of the forest and saw

The Recipient

Kiandra approaching on her horse. The look on her face said it all.

Lucifer was now in open rebellion.

This meant war.

Nothing would ever be the same.

The Recipient

Chapter two

The Wild Card

Small town Americana in the 1970's: A little bundle of
energy with blonde hair and a spark of life in his eyes
made a dash for the biggest slide in the park. He loved
the feel of running fast. It made him feel like a super-
hero. He climbed up to the top and felt like the king of
the playground. From his perch he looked up and
thought, *I wonder if I can see heaven from here*. Five-
year-old boys have lots of questions. They also have
short attention spans. He slid down and made a mad
dash for a peculiarly shaped oak tree. The huge knot in
it made it easier to climb. He launched himself up the
tree and scrambled up to a branch, then the next one.
"Bear! You're going too high!" He heard his mom shout
from the front porch. "Oh, let him go. He's a boy." Said
Bear's Dad, walking to the house from the pole barn.
"Boys climb trees."

After supper Bear walked into the living room, where
the Brady Bunch was on TV. He liked watching the
show, but he was getting distracted. His eyes kept
drifting to the left side of the green plaid couch. It didn't
look any different, but it seemed different. Strange. He
cocked his head like he had seen the dog do many
times. Maybe that helped the brain process thoughts
better. Something was drawing him to that spot. He
stuck his hand in between the cushions and felt around.
He found something small and hard, and pulled it out. It
was a diamond ring! He ran outside with a big smile on

his face, "Mom! I found your ring!" Bear's mom smiled at him as she took the ring from him and put it on her finger. She asked, "Where did you find it?" Bear took her to the living room and showed her where he found it. This sort of thing happened occasionally, but he didn't tell his mom *everything*. She might not understand.

Around three o'clock that night Bear woke up terrified. He tried to call for help, but nothing came out. He was afraid to open his eyes. He tried to get out of bed, but he couldn't move. After what seemed like an eternity, his legs started working again, so he jumped out of bed and ran to his parent's bedroom. "Mom!" Her eyes snapped open and fastened on Bear. "What is it, Bear?" She saw that familiar fear in his eyes, and said, "Is it her?" Bear didn't say anything; he just nodded. The lady in red was back again. Every so often Bear would have a nightmare of a frozen lady in a red dress that was behind the refrigerator. His mom wondered if it was because of the previous owners of the house. There were rumors that he was an alcoholic, and whatever nightmarish things happened there, stayed in the walls of the house. Meanwhile, Bear's dad was stirring from sleep. He sat up and saw Bear. "Why are you up?" He asked. Bear hung his head and mumbled, "Nightmare." His dad reacted brusquely, "Go back to bed. Nightmares can't hurt you. Besides, I've got a shotgun right here." He reached down and patted the double-barrel shotgun near his bed. "Anything gets in here – I'll take care of it."

Standing nearby, yet invisible to the members of this family, were Kiandra and Zavan, who noted, "His gift puts him in danger." Kiandra replied, "Being a seer is a privilege, but it does carry with it certain amount of peril." They both understood clearly that there were no guarantees while living in a fallen world. "Yes, the greater the potential for good, the more attention he gets from the enemy. So, you're going to have your hands full."

The 1980's

The distinct smell of wrestling mats, Ben Gay and sweat filled the air as Bear was practicing his takedowns – he called it 'shadow wrestling'. He liked working on his technique after everyone else had gone. There was a comforting familiarity about this room. He felt more secure here than in the halls of the school or the classrooms. The door opened and the janitor pushed his cart into the room. "Hey kid, why don't you hit the shower? I have to clean up." Bear nodded his head and walked out past a poster of Dan Gable in his prime executing a perfect five-point throw. Bear looked at the poster and wondered to himself, *how do you become a legend? Does it take more than hard work? Passion? Luck? I wonder if I'll ever inspire anyone.* Then he heard himself say out loud, "What good am I?" He stopped for a second, wondering where that came from. *That got dark fast,* He thought.

Lurking nearby, unseen by human eyes, was a sinister figure with a hint of satisfaction registering on his face. It was Dagon. In his centuries of never-ending conflict, he had learned to deal with potential problems before they became actual problems. Whenever he sensed that someone had a potential for greatness in the army of light, he would begin a well-orchestrated attack designed to neutralize the effectiveness of the subject, turn them to the dark side, or just destroy them. No one was too young to attack; in fact, he preferred them young and vulnerable. It made his job easier.

"I wish you'd eat more," Bear's mom said, watching him eat a small pile of peas and a little turkey. He replied, "The state qualifier is coming up, Mom. I have to drop some weight. If I win the state tournament, or even place well, it could land me that scholarship to Iowa State." His mom said, "I know you really want to get into their architectural program, but I don't like to see you starving yourself." At that moment Bear's dad came in, and Mom asked him how his day was. His response was a curt, "Oh, you know – like any other. How did you match go tonight, Bear?" Bear's eyes brightened a little and said, "I beat him 7 to 3! He was ranked 6th in the state." Dad responded without even thinking, "Why didn't you pin him?" Bear quickly looked down to his plate to avoid showing what his eyes revealed. Bear's dad sensed the tension, glanced at his wife, took a breath like he was going to say something, but instead walked out of the room. Bear's dad was the definition of old school. He loved his family and was a good provider. He would die for them in a heartbeat, but revealing any emotion was a whole different matter.

As Bear was standing in the doorway of his bedroom wondering if he should go back to the kitchen and find something to eat or just ignore his stomach growling, he suddenly saw himself in another place. He could still see his bedroom and everything around him, but he could also see another scene – like a dream, except he wasn't asleep. He watched himself, dressed in a mailman's uniform, approach a table in a foyer with a package on it. This package was small enough to carry, and it was decorated like a Christmas present. It was wrapped with shiny paper that changed color, from purple to green to mauve, depending on how the light hit it. The bow was no less amazing, with four loops that had diamond chips fastened on them. *If the wrapping is that ornate, the gift itself must be amazing!* He picked it up, and the scene changed. Now he was in a shopping mall, carrying the present. He was weaving in and out of the shoppers, looking for the person who was supposed to receive the gift. Somehow, he knew it was very important to get that gift to the intended recipient. He also knew that when he found the right person, he would just know. Then, poof! It was over, and he was back looking at his bedroom. *What in the world was that all about?*

The Recipient

The Recipient

Chapter three

Down to Earth

After siding with Lucifer and joining the rebellion,
Dagon found out that it's not a good idea to
underestimate the creator. As Kiandra had told Zavan,
he keeps an eye on everything. Lucifer and his followers
quickly lost the battle for the third heaven, and were
banished to earth. He became obsessed with revenge.
Dagon could see that Lucifer wasn't in control anymore
– something had captured and possessed him. Evil now
had a home. And a name: Satan, the first orphan.
Because he cut himself off from the Father, he needed
to create a purpose for his existence. He became his
purpose. His ambition became his mission. He organized
a hierarchy and continued his campaign against the
creator, but this time he went about it more
strategically. He knew he couldn't win a direct battle, so
he targeted the object of the creator's affection:
humans. There was no manual for corrupting mankind,
so he had to figure it out from scratch. He decided
against openly presenting himself as the better
alternative to Elohim, as he had previously attempted.
That would be too honest. Deception became his
primary tool. His most effective ploy was to convince
the humans that he didn't even exist.

Dagon proved himself useful to Lucifer, with his vast
knowledge of eternal law, and advanced quickly
through the ranks. All the strategies they developed
focused on two goals: either harming humans directly

or turning them against the creator. He found that humans would pay nearly anything to obtain secret knowledge. He discovered loopholes in eternal law, and became one of the most successful traffickers of information on earth: energy sources, spells for mind control, secrets of longevity, even love potions – people would literally sell their souls for power. It was almost too easy.

One of Lucifer's most spectacular successes came through a loophole in eternal law that allowed fallen angels to cloak themselves in human-like flesh, including the ability to reproduce. He convinced a great number of fallen angels to commit to the course of polluting the human genome, ultimately to prevent the birth of the messiah, who needed to have a pure human bloodline. The result of this unholy union between humans and celestials was a hybrid race called Nephilim, who possessed unusual powers, and often great size and strength. Many of them became rulers and were worshiped as gods, and filled the earth will fear and violence. If the trend wasn't stopped, mankind would have been completely wiped out. It appeared that Lucifer's control of earth was absolute, but he didn't count on the creator implementing a drastic countermove. He chose a man named Noah, who was one of the last men on earth with a purely human bloodline. He and his family were given the mission of saving what was worth being saved from the coming flood. He accomplished his mission, and Lucifer's plan was thwarted, at least temporarily.

The Recipient

It was approximately 1090 BC in the near east, in a region called Canaan, or Philistia, and Dagon's reign had begun. Through many centuries of deception, treachery and manipulation, he was now being worshipped as a deity. He was Dagon, the Philistine fish-god that rose from the Great Sea. Now he could demand human sacrifices. Blood was always the goal, and blood meant power. The expansion of his empire was in view, particularly south and east. To subjugate Israel was a great prize for any fallen angel. There was a problem, though: an upstart, the Israeli strongman named Samson, who was preventing him from capturing Israel. Dagon was sure that this human was getting help from the third heaven.

Dagon learned that there was a great deal of enemy activity at the Judean plateau, so he went there to find out for himself. When he got there, he sensed it – a presence he had not felt in a very long time. There was also a smell – a fragrance he used to enjoy, but now was unbearable. It burned his nostrils. It was unmistakably the scent of the third heaven. "It really is a small world…" The voice of Zavan brought back an avalanche of unwanted memories. He turned in the direction of the voice to see the same angel he had known so well eons ago. He looked the same, except that he seemed to carry himself differently. Zavan now had a confidence that was undeniable. Dagon's eyes narrowed, "What are you doing in my territory?" "No salutation for your old friend?" Zavan taunted. Dagon was in no mood this.

The Recipient

"I have the right to be here, and you know it. We have the title deed to the earth – handed over to Lucifer by a *human*." Zavan replied, "I tried to warn you – you chose poorly." Changing the subject, Dagon stated, "I am being worshipped by an entire nation. You know what that means to my claim on this land." Zavan knew that he was telling the truth, but he also knew that the creator had a habit of turning around impossible situations by unleashing key people at strategic times. This was one of those times. There was so much he could have told Dagon, but all he said was, "There will be a confrontation, and you will lose." Before Dagon could say another word, Zavan vanished.

Zavan wrote in his journal: *I am overwhelmed by such a tremendous burden – I have failed. I was given the duty to protect Samson and help him carry out his mission. I had such great hope for him. He could have been the greatest judge in Israel's history. He could have permanently defeated the Philistines, and his legacy would have endured for generations. I was unable to deter him from his own human frailties. For all his great strength, he was still just a man with vulnerabilities. Ego. Lust. Dagon knew his weaknesses and capitalized on them. Samson killed thousands of enemy soldiers but was destroyed by a woman! No, in truth, he was destroyed by his own lust. I will avenge Samson. Dagon will pay for this.*

The Recipient

Energized by the death of Samson, Dagon continued his quest for dominance. He understood the value of relics, not just in regard to the motivational aspects of symbolism, but in raw spiritual power. "Zavan will find out soon that the Philistine army has just captured the Ark of the Covenant – the very presence of the creator on earth. This will be my greatest victory yet!" At that moment the Ark of the Covenant was being carried into the temple in Ashdod to sit in front of Dagon's statue, signifying Dagon's dominance. He added, "Now the Philistines and the Israelis will all see who is more powerful! I will reign for a thousand years!"

The next morning Dagon and the people of Ashdod were shocked to see that Dagon's statue had fallen down before the Ark. The news spread like wildfire, and the people's confidence in Dagon had been shaken. He knew his reign couldn't survive another hit like this. "Dagon." The voice came from someone he knew well, but the tone of his voice spoke volumes – this was not a social call. "Baasha", said Dagon, and bowed low. "To what do I owe this honor?" asked Dagon, barely containing his contempt for his superior. "I won't mince words. After this incident, you are holding on by a thread." Baasha continued, "This incident sent shock waves through the second heaven." Dagon interjected, "I assure you -" but Baasha cut him off. "I do not need your assurances! I need you to hold on to your power. Do what you must – or you will be banished."

A short time later, Zavan once again made his way into the temple in Ashdod unnoticed by humans or celestials. He was grateful for the cover provided by the

Israelis who remained faithful to Elohim – without them his mission would have been nearly impossible. He got behind the statue of Dagon and pushed. As the statue began to topple, he guided its fall so the head and hands of the statue snapped off. Zavan knew that occult practitioners relied heavily on symbolism. Cutting off the hands and head meant a loss of authority. This would be the end for Dagon.

The Recipient

Chapter four

Regrets

The aroma of eggs and sausage filled the kitchen of the century-plus old farmhouse. It had been updated several times, but still had its country charm. Bear was cooking breakfast in a cast iron skillet. His routine didn't vary much. He heard his phone beep, so he picked it up and looked at it and found his first appointment of the day. An estimate for a new bay window. *A new bay window – be still, my wildly beating heart. I know – sarcasm doesn't become me. It is what it is. It's honest work.*

Bear knew he had to keep a tight rein on his mind, or it would wander off to what could have been, threatening to pull him into that dark pit of discouragement. He wasn't always successful, though. He went over to his desk and noticed an old photo album, which he opened and saw a couple newspaper clippings. The first one had a picture of him back in the day during a wrestling match, with the caption: 'McQuade has shot at Iowa State scholarship'. He pulled out the other clipping, which read: 'Accident sidelines local wrestler'. Before he could stop his thoughts, they drifted back decades. It was like he was watching a film on an old 8-millimeter projector. His buddy Wade had come to pick him up to study for their science test. It wasn't Wade's fault; the other car came flying out of nowhere and T-boned them on the passenger's side. It wasn't until much later Bear realized that he had been knocked unconscious for several minutes. Bear heard through the grapevine that the driver was a young man from a wealthy family, and alcohol may have been involved. The whole ordeal seemed like a lifetime away. *So much for the scholarship and the wrestling career.* Bear was being assaulted by his thoughts: *My life wasn't supposed to go like this. I was supposed to become an architect and be happily married by now. What about the guy that plowed into me? Did he ever pay a price for what he did?*

After breakfast Bear went out to attend to his horse, Dusty, who was inside the older-than-dirt barn. The siding at one time had been painted barn red, but now was a weathered gray color. Bear hadn't yet decided whether to repaint it or burn the whole thing down and start over. Bear leaned against Dusty and stared out over the pasture, lost in thought. He spent a lot of time in his head. It looked like the thousand-yard stare he used to do back when he was competing. Call it a vision or just an overactive imagination, Bear saw in his mind's eye a bright shaft of light coming down from the sky. He was a little uncomfortable with the whole concept of mystery – that meant he wasn't in control. Just then his horse stomped its foot to get rid of a pesky horsefly that wouldn't get the hint, which snapped Bear out of his thoughts. He had picked up Dusty for a song because his left front hoof was split, and it wasn't healing very well. Bear kept it wrapped up and used a generous amount of salve to help it heal. He had a soft spot in his heart for horses, especially this one. He picked up Dusty's hoof to examine it. "How's your hoof doing, buddy?" It almost seemed like the horse understood what he was saying. They just seemed to connect. Bear continued, "It's nice to take care of someone who appreciates it. You'll never stab me in the back, right?" Bear's eyes narrowed a little and said, "Well, maybe that's because you don't have fingers." Dusty shook his head. It was uncanny – like he really understood what Bear was saying. Or maybe he was just picking up on the vibes – like animals sometimes do. Bear noticed and said, "Just kidding, Bud."

Bear went into the back part of the shed, where rays of light illuminated the dusty air. He didn't spend much time there – the musty smell made him feel too closed in. He went over to an old junked-out 1970 convertible coupe and sat in what was left of the driver's seat. Bear sometimes talked to the car. It wasn't like he was expecting an answer, but sometimes words just need to be spoken. "Why did I buy you?" He turned his right ear toward the dash as if to hear better. "What's that? You had potential? Well, that and a quarter will get me a phone call." Bear sat in silence for a moment. "You're all beat up. You've been through the meat grinder. Are you even worth my time? What good are you?" Those words sounded strangely familiar, but he couldn't put his finger on the time or place.

But life goes on. Happiness, busy-ness, misery, numbness... life just goes on. Bear went back into the house after doing a few pullups, which was part of his morning routine.

The Recipient

Bear drove up to the house for his first appointment and walked up the door of a quaint rambler that had been built before Bear had been born. It opened right away, and a man in his sixties greeted him, "I'm Dan - You must be Bear." "Yes sir", Bear smiled, and shook the man's hand. When their hands touched, time stopped for a moment, and Bear saw a vision... an alternative reality... he didn't know what to call it. Inside the chest cavity of his new prospect he could see a glass heart that appeared to be cracked. Dan suddenly dropped to the ground and sobbed uncontrollably. The vision ended as abruptly as it began - back to reality – they were shaking hands, and Dan was just fine. He said, "Come on in. This is my wife Karen." After they exchanged pleasantries, they showed Bear the window in their dining room that they wanted to be replaced with a new bay window. He went through his sales pitch, being careful not to call it a sales pitch. "This won't take long – maybe two days max. Let me give you a call when I get the details together." He would get back to them with a final price and the paperwork in a couple days. Paperwork. That's what he was trained to call it. Not a contract. The official phrase was to 'execute the contract', but that terminology would send the average prospect running away in terror, so they just refer to it as 'paperwork'.

As they were walking toward the front door, Bear noticed an American flag folded next to the picture of a young marine. He focused on it just long enough for Karen to notice. She put her hand on Dan's shoulder and said, "Dan's son Marty didn't make it back from Iraq." Bear swallowed hard and said to Dan, who was looking at the floor, "I'm very sorry."

Bear walked back to his truck and turned around and looked at the house. The handyman business is just as much about people as it is about fixing stuff. Every now and then you run into a situation that book learning doesn't prepare you for. Fixing stuff is easy. Fixing people – not so much.

Healing broken hearts is God's business, not mine. But why would he show me that if I couldn't help?

Bear's thoughts were interrupted by the sound of a baby crying in a park across the street. On any other day, the sound of a baby crying wouldn't get his attention, but this didn't feel like a regular day. It felt like a day to break out of his normal routine, so he followed the sound. It led to a park bench a stone's throw from a basketball court where a half dozen kids were shooting hoops. On the bench was a disheveled young woman holding the crying baby whose eyes were red from crying herself. Bear felt compelled to approach her. "Tough day?" The woman looked at Bear. "He won't stop crying. I don't know what else to do." Bear noticed a tingling sensation in his right hand that hadn't been there a minute ago. After hesitating for a moment, he asked, "Can I try?" The woman looked at him with skepticism in her eyes. Bear knew very well that normally a mother would never let a stranger hold her baby. But today was not a normal day. Maybe she was desperate, or maybe she could see in his eyes that he was sincere. Maybe she believed that he had been sent there to help her. Whatever the reason, she stood up and gingerly handed over her wailing little bundle. Bear cradled him in his left arm and put his right hand on the baby's head, then closed his eyes. Within about twenty seconds the crying had stopped. As he handed him back to the woman, she said, "You must be a father." He immediately turned around a walked away, not wanting to reveal the pain registering on his face.

He could keep on ignoring it, like he usually did, or he could face those old memories – maybe he could finally get some closure and move on. Bear's heart raced as he walked through the barn, and his focus landed on an old motorcycle shrouded with canvas, obviously unused for quite some time. The projector began to play again on the theater of his mind:

"Come on honey, let's go for a quick ride. You know I'm a good driver." The young woman hesitated, looking at the motorcycle, then put her hand on her abdomen. She was barely showing. Bear was in a good mood, feeling invincible, and persuasive. She agreed to go for a ride with him. Bear ignored that quiet voice whispering to him that this was not a good idea. They got to the second curve in the road, when a six-point buck darted out in front of them. There was no time to swerve. No time to do anything.

The Recipient

Next stop was the hospital. Even though he felt like he was in a daze, it was forever etched in his memory – especially when the doctor came out to talk to him. He was dressed in scrubs with thick gray hair and horn-rimmed glasses. And the hospital smell – ever since that day Bear couldn't stand the smell of disinfectant. The doctor's face said it all. They lost the baby.

He remembered the graveyard, seeing the little grave marker, and wishing it could have been him in the ground instead of the baby. He didn't even make an attempt to justify himself. He was guilty.

How do you ever come back from that? If God has a plan, he better get on with it.

Although Bear felt more alone than he had ever been, he was not alone. He was being observed by an unseen ally. Zavan wrote in his journal as he watched the situation unfold on his monitor:

I'll never forget that day either. I tried to warn him. He was just caught up in the moment.

I wondered if he was close to ending it all. How do you console someone who is inconsolable? How do I get him through this?

Zavan looked around his office through the glass walls and windows that gave him a superb view of the city and his co-workers who were busy with their duties. Zavan was ferociously loyal and determined to do whatever was necessary to help his charge.

The Recipient

Chapter five

Starting over

Circa 1340 AD

How long have I been here? Dagon wondered to himself. *It's been well over two thousand years since Baasha banished me from Philistia. If not for Zavan's interference… How I hate that name. He defeated me without even a battle. Next time… If I ever see him again, it will be different.*

Dagon was still furious about his fall from prominence, and was determined to rebuild his empire, even if he only had a few backward savages to influence. His work had been largely unchallenged, and the creator was practically unheard of in this area. Dagon was determined to keep his enemy from establishing an outpost in this region. He gradually introduced the natives to his brand of sorcery, initially by guiding them to identify with dogs as their spirit animal. Dagon knew their reverence for nature and their penchant for symbology, and capitalized on it. Anything to keep their focus off the creator. He trained them to open their spirits to the canine mystique. Whenever they saw a wolf, a coyote, a fox… it would create a psychological anchor that would bind them even deeper to the occult practice. He had to congratulate himself for his brilliance for coming up with that angle. He also taught some of his disciples the skill of invading dreams and altered states of consciousness. A few of them had become so advanced as to gain the power of shape shifting – they were called 'skinwalkers'. The practice was so feared that even talking about it was forbidden. Through many centuries of trafficking in secrets, he had managed to develop an unbroken line of occult practice, forming what he believed was an impenetrable shield over his kingdom.

It was time. Dagon had desensitized his followers over several generations, to the point where they would obey his command to shed human blood and offer it to him.

He walked into the dark, windowless stone chamber. It was twenty three paces to the granite throne that was in the center of the room. He climbed the throne and sat down. It was eerily quiet for several minutes. Dagon closed his eyes and repeated, "I saw Satan fall like lightning. I saw Satan fall like lightning. I saw Satan fall like lightning." Soon the red liquid oozed down the walls and into channels that had been cut in the floor. As it flowed to a basin in the center of the room just in front of the throne, Dagon could feel the energy swirling around him. He breathed deeply and received the power that was being offered to him. In spite of their complete and utter obedience to him, Dagon felt (as did all the fallen angels) nothing but a smoldering contempt for his followers. He despised them, yet they worshiped him. No matter how much they offered, his bloodlust was never satisfied. He wanted to push them; to test the limits of their devotion. At what point would the creator push back? Deep down he knew it wouldn't last forever.

The Recipient

Present day:

Speeding around a curve in a shiny midnight blue late model BMW, Dagon checked his watch to make sure he would be on time for the emergency meeting he had been summoned to. He had no problem taking full advantage of new technology as it became available. It made him that much more efficient. Human nature hadn't changed – people were still eager to gain power at any cost, but the enemy had also made inroads. He had been feeling the pushback. There was tension in the air that he couldn't explain. Maybe he would get some answers at the meeting.

Dagon pulled up to an iron gate near a guard shack and rolled down the window. He took off his sunglasses and looked at the guard, who nodded and opened the gate. He drove up to a huge European style mansion that hinted at old money. The sprawling estate had been passed down from heir to heir since the 1830's, and had been their usual meeting place the entire time.

Wearing a dramatic full-length black trench coat, Dagon got out of his car, attracting the attention of the guard dogs - two intimidating Rottweilers who stayed clear of him as soon as they saw who he was. He walked up to the oak double doors, which opened automatically. He strode into a huge foyer with at least a thirty-foot ceiling with circular marble staircases on each side. He walked down a long hall and opened the door into a large, dimly lit room paneled with dark wood from floor to ceiling. In the center was an oblong table with fourteen people seated around it. At the head of the table was Baasha, wearing an impatient look: "The meeting is now convened." Dagon took the only remaining seat. He recognized everyone around the table. They were all ancient, all celestial, with a humorless look on every face. Baasha continued, "I felt it was necessary to call this meeting, given the information we have just learned..." Dagon scowled, knowing Baasha's infuriating tendency to grandstand. Baasha droned on and on, but eventually got to the point. "You may have heard rumors, but we have confirmed it – the enemy has plans to open up a portal from the third heaven." The room erupted in chaos. Everyone was shouting at once, asking questions, wondering who to blame. "Order!" bellowed Baasha. The room quieted down, and Dagon spoke up. "What is the location?" Baasha answered, "The exact location is unknown, but we believe it's planned for your region." The words hit Dagon like a club. His mouth went dry as his thoughts reverted back to his humiliating loss in Ashdod. Baasha went on, "I called all of you here because if it is successfully opened, it will affect all of you." One of the beings at the table asked, "Do we know who has been chosen to open the portal? Because unless I've missed something, it takes a human working in conjunction with the enemy to open one." Baasha answered, "You've each been given an envelope – all the information you need is inside." They all tore open the envelopes and began scanning the documents. A large, gnarled creature wearing a hood said, "They must be scraping the bottom of the barrel." Dagon retorted, "Don't be naïve – we've all been fooled by appearances before."

The Recipient

Baasha pushed a button on a control panel at the head of the table and the lights dimmed, then a hologram began materializing in the middle of the table. As the figure became clearer, Dagon felt every muscle in his body tighten up. It was a three-dimensional image of Zavan, rotating clockwise. Baasha looked at Dagon, who was regaining his composure, and said in a condescending tone, "I believe you're familiar with Zavan." Dagon chose to play it cool, and remarked, "We have history. What does he have to do with the portal?" Baasha answered, "According to our sources, he has been chosen to run point on this operation. If you require backup" – Dagon exploded, "I CAN HANDLE ZAVAN!" Everyone looked at him for a moment, then Baasha refocused their attention back to the image in the center of the table. The hologram changed to another individual that Dagon also knew. "This one is known as Bear McQuade. We don't believe he is the recipient, but he could play an important role in this operation. It could be nothing or it could mean trouble." Dagon interjected, "I've been keeping an eye on him. I'll run interference as necessary. I'm not terribly concerned about him right now." In an ominous tone, Baasha commented, "If he discovers his potential, I don't think I need to spell out what that means for us." The hooded figure chimed in, "According to his dossier, he has no interest in his prophetic gift. It's unclear if he even knows there is a war going on. But if he obtains the stones of fire"- Baasha immediately cut him off, "There's no need to speculate!" Turning the focus back on Dagon, he said, "This forerunner *must* be neutralized. Now, are you up to this?" Dagon was seething inside; he knew Baasha wanted to bring up his past failure at the hands of Zavan just to humiliate him. He spat back through clenched teeth, *"I will handle it."* Baasha added ominously, "We will be watching."

Another participant asked the question that everyone was thinking but no one wanted to ask: "How much time do we have to prepare?" Baasha hesitated and said, "Our information is a little sketchy on the timing." He took off his glasses and continued, "We don't know." The hooded figure exploded, "You mean it could happen today?" Dagon added "Or fifty years from now." Baasha closed with, "The enemy is never in a hurry. You all know what to do. Get busy."

In his cavern-like lair, Dagon was pacing back and forth like a caged beast. He walked into an adjacent room just off the main area; it was empty except for a small table with a computer and a pair of unusual-looking goggles on it. He put on the goggles, and immediately saw the 3D computer-generated images in the room: it had been transformed into a high-tech manhunt headquarters. Dagon had been working on this for quite some time. One entire wall had been turned into a bulletin board containing photos and biographies of the people he had been researching: Bear McQuade, Jennifer, Missy... along with dozens of others. There were research articles pinned up, connected to other articles and pictures by various colored threads. There were hundreds of hand-written notes scribbled everywhere. On the other walls were symbols and artifacts, connected to other images by threads – all done in virtual reality.

Dagon needed to find a vulnerability. An opening. He double-tapped a file icon on his cyber-screen, and it opened up into yet another file. He drew a red line from it to Jennifer's picture, then jotted down a note. His eyes darted back and forth as a plan started to form. He quickly scrolled down a list of names on a computer screen, then stopped on a name. He threw it up onto a larger screen, then expanded the picture, and stared at the man onscreen. Reece Bernell's background couldn't be better: Rich... Handsome... Ruthless... His eyes were cold. He was Perfect.

The Recipient

The Recipient

Chapter six

Mystery Man

Bear had just gone into his barn to get his post hole digger, when he detected the distinct smell of roses. He looked around to see where it was coming from, but didn't see any flowers. Why would flowers be in his barn, anyway? He thought maybe his nose was playing tricks on him, but the smell got stronger. He stopped what he was doing, then everything went black, and a spotlight lit up the ground right in front of him, getting brighter and brighter. It illuminated a table covered by a white tablecloth, with a small object in the center. He felt no fear, only curiosity, so he approached it. It was a glass heart, like the one he saw in the vision with Dan, his hopefully soon-to-be client. He could see it had the same cracks in it. He picked up the heart and held it with both hands, and as he was looking at it, his hands started to heat up and the heart began to glow. Bear's heart started to beat faster. *What's going on? Am I supposed to be doing this?* As he was trying to absorb what was happening, he noticed that the cracks in the heart were being erased, as if time were going backwards. He could see the lines disappearing before his eyes. The light started to dim, and he found himself back in his barn, with everything just as it was. *What was that all about?* He didn't have much time to think about it – he heard the sound of a vehicle coming down the driveway.

The Recipient

It sounded like Neal's Hummer H2. Neal had told him he was going to stop over after work. How do you describe Neal but a walking contradiction? A sophisticated redneck. Neal was a high-powered attorney sporting long-ish brown hair and a good deal of face fuzz. He looked like he belonged on the cover of Outdoor Life. He spoke with a good-ole-boy southern drawl and liked fine whiskey - not the cheap stuff. He considered his redneck appearance his disguise. His courtroom opponents never took him seriously. They never saw him coming, and that's the way he liked it.

Bear remembered how they met – just a routine interior remodeling job on an upscale house in a ritzy suburb. They started talking and hit it off. He liked how Bear didn't try to upsell him or try too hard to get him to sign right away. Neal lived in a world of fast-talking slicksters who would sell their own mothers if the price was right. He had gotten used to watching his own back and not trusting people, but he could tell right away there was something different about Bear.

You didn't need to be a prophet to know that Neal wasn't from around here. He wasn't one to open up about his past, though – even to Bear. If that subject came up, Neal would find a way to redirect the conversation. He was a lawyer; he was good at talking.

The Hummer parked with its back end facing the barn where Bear was. He noticed the new lettering all across the back of the massive vehicle: NO APOLOGIES. Yeah, that pretty much summed up Neal. He opened the door and stepped out in all his backwoods glory: faded jeans, checkered button-down shirt, belt buckle and cowboy hat. Bear greeted him with, "Welcome to rancho de Bear! You're late." Neal shot back, "I heard something about a beer with my name on it, so here I am." Bear pulled out two cold bottles from a cooler by his feet. Bear said, "I have a wine cooler in case that's more your thing." Neal rolled his eyes and shot back, "No thanks, dude – I have testicles." Bear laughed and said, "Come on, let's check it out. This way." They both walked into the shed. After laying eyes on it, Neal said, "Nice! That's a classic." Bear replied, "I bought him to restore, but everyone who sees him thinks he's too far gone." Neal commented thoughtfully, "It would take a lot of work. That would be a labor of love." Bear agreed, "That it would. I sure wouldn't do it to make a profit. It would have to be just the satisfaction of taking something worthless and making it valuable." Neal ran his fingers over the hood, "So what's the verdict? Are you gonna go for it?" Bear thought for a second, "I'm having second thoughts. I'm wondering if some things are just not restorable."

A few minutes later the two were in lawn chairs with their feet up on the fence hoisting their respective beverages, and watching Dusty as he was feeling his oats, galloping around the pasture.

Neal: "Okay, Lynyrd Skynyrd or Creedence Clearwater Revival?"

Bear: "Are you kidding? Skynyrd all the way!"

They clinked their bottles together, then took a swig.

Bear: "All right – Earth, Wind and Fire or Chicago?

Neal: "I saw Earth, Wind and Fire live back in the day – best concert ever!"

Bear: "They're in a class by themselves!"

Neal: "Now if you're into the cryin' in the beer music, Chicago might be more your style. You know what I learned, though – never listen to Chicago Sixteen after you go through a breakup."

Bear: "The lawyer makes a good point."

There were a few moments of silence as they watched the sun begin to set, causing Dusty to appear to take on a richer hue.

Neal: "Last one: The Eagles or Bachman Turner Overdrive?"

Bear: "Got to go with The Eagles."

Neal: "Are you kidding? BTO is legendary!"

Bear: "I guess there's no accounting for taste."

Neal: "Dude! We're talking raw talent here."

Bear: "Hey Ty! Come here!"

Ty, a teenager from the neighborhood who liked horses, and had sort of a nephew-uncle relationship with Bear, had been working on the other side of the barn, walked over to the two, curious about what he was getting into. He looked at Bear inquisitively. Bear said, "We need you to settle a debate. The Eagles or Bachman Turner Overdrive?" Ty looked at them and shook his head.

The Recipient

"Maroon 5." Both Bear and Neal said in unison, "Who?" Ty just rolled his eyes and walked away.

After Neal and Ty were gone, Bear went back into the house, hoping he could cross a few things off his list before he called it a day. He pulled on a bookshelf in his living room, and it swung out like a door, revealing an opening. He walked through it into a windowless room about the size of a small bedroom. On one entire side were shelves that ran the whole length of the room with supplies: jugs of water, canned food, buckets, tools and gadgets. On the other side was a couch, with blankets and pillows, and a single light hung from the ceiling. It looked like a doomsday room or a tinfoil hat prepper room. Bear installed a cover plate on an electric outlet and fastened it in place while thinking, *maybe I'm paranoid. I don't like calling it a panic room, but it sure doesn't hurt to be prepared.* He pulled up the security feed on a tablet to make sure the cameras were working, and he could see what was going on. Front porch camera, check; living room camera, check; driveway camera, check. A wave of fatigue swept over him, as he realized he had been working longer than he thought. He got ready for bed, and it seemed like he was out before his head even hit the pillow.

Bear was in a dark room and could barely see anything until a door cracked open just a bit on the other side. A brilliant light shone through the opening. Whatever was behind that door was intense! He took a step toward it, then hesitated. It felt like a tug of war between fear and curiosity. Thoughts volleyed back and forth in his mind.

Instead of going in, he turned around and felt the wall in the darkness for an exit.

Bear's eyes snapped open - he was in bed. It took a few seconds for him to get his bearings. *Okay, I'm in my room...* A shaft of moonlight shone through the window, illuminating his billfold and some change on the dresser. He also a pile of receipts and bills on the table. The top one was job 3314. Ordinarily he wouldn't think twice about it, but something caught his attention. He flipped on the light and grabbed his Bible from the shelf, opened it to Job chapter 33, verse 14, and read in a whisper, *"For God speaks again and again, though people do not recognize it. He speaks in dreams, in visions of the night, when deep sleep falls on people as they lie in their beds."*

The Recipient

Chapter seven

Point of No Return

Jennifer was sitting on an expensive maroon leather couch in the great room in front of the fireplace, sipping a glass of chardonnay. She was the consummate trophy wife: long, full blonde hair, delicate jawline and big brown eyes with only a hint of aging. She wanted to believe she had married well.

The whole south side of the great room was floor to ceiling windows, letting the sunlight flood into the entire space. She closed her eyes to feel the warmth of the sun on her face, trying to enjoy it, but something was gnawing at her. She knew it was there, but she just kept shoving it to the back of her mind. Things were going too well to let unwelcome thoughts ruin everything. It was time to plan her day.

I should be able to squeeze in a manicure after my workout at the spa if I drop off Missy a little early to her violin practice. If I had Reece pick her up afterwards, I could get some shopping in. Jennifer felt a twinge of uneasiness when it came to Reece spending time with Missy. How could she not trust her new husband? Her eyes wandered around the exquisite room and landed on a picture sitting on the end table. She picked it up and studied it. It was the first time Reece invited her to go sailing on his yacht. They were the perfect couple, all smiles, with the ocean in the background. She put it back and picked up the one next to it – taken on their wedding day as they were about to take the jet to Tel

The Recipient

Aviv for their honeymoon. Their wedding day - just a few months ago. It really had been a whirlwind romance, like something out of a romance novel. She had never been wined and dined like that before. Reece knew how to impress a woman, but exactly who was this man she had married? She got up and went into Reece's den, hoping to get more insight into him. Part of her didn't want to know more; just enjoy the good life and don't ask too many questions. The other part of her knew that sooner or later she would have to ask those questions, and the longer she waited, the more fallout there would be. Her curious side won, so she looked around the spacious room, wondering why he collected weapons. Among those on display there was a German Ruger from World War II, a pair of Samurai swords from ancient Japan, a curved dagger with what appeared to be an emerald embedded in the handle, and exotic weapons she didn't even recognize. Must be a guy thing.

She went back to the kitchen to pour herself another glass of wine. She had never been to Reece's warehouse. She wasn't even sure what he did for a living. Whatever it was, he was doing a bang-up job, because money was never a problem. She thought back to their conversations – he hardly ever talked about his work, although she remembered him saying something about import/export something or other. Shouldn't a wife know about her husband's work?

Jennifer thought back to when they met. It was a chance meeting at a high-class bar. She remembered sitting at the bar, dressed to the nines, finishing a strawberry margarita. It felt like fate. Reece seemed to appear out of nowhere, although he had been watching her for a few minutes. "I need to buy you a drink." Came the voice from behind her. As she turned around on the barstool, she met eyes with a good-looking man in a perfectly tailored Italian suit, with his tie loosened up a bit. "My name is Reece, by the way." She remembered being immediately drawn to his confidence.

"Mom, it's time to go!" Missy called out, snapping Jennifer out of her trip down memory lane. "Okay, honey, I'll meet you at the car."

As they buckled themselves into her white Corvette, Jennifer asked, "You did remember your violin, right?" Missy smiled, "Of course, Mom!" and pointed behind the seat, where it was tucked away. Mrs. Steever says it won't be long before she won't be able to teach me anymore. She says I'll be too advanced." Jennifer heard herself say out loud, "I wonder where you got your talent from; it sure wasn't from me." "Maybe it was from my dad." Missy said, as she met eyes with Jennifer, who hurriedly shifted the car into drive and sped away and asked, "Is it okay if Reece picks you up after violin practice?" Missy just shrugged her shoulders.

After she dropped Missy off, Jennifer breathed a little sigh of relief. Missy had never met her father. Jennifer struggled with telling her what happened. Her dad wasn't in the picture, period. It was clear that Missy needed him. There was a big void in her life, like an elephant in the room that nobody talked about. Now that the subject was out there, Jennifer had to rethink the whole story. *What should I tell her now? She's not a little girl anymore. She deserves some answers. I still hope Reece can fill that void.* She didn't want to think about this stuff anymore. *It's all so complicated. I thought money was supposed to make life easier. I need a break from all this. Spa, here I come.*

The next morning as Jennifer descended the grandiose circular stairs while in her plush microfiber bathrobe, Missy was already up, playing on her tablet. Reece was... somewhere, probably in his den. She hadn't seen him. The sound of the doorbell chime filled the foyer, and Jennifer called out, "I got it", to nobody in particular. She opened the door to see Amy, Missy's friend from down the street. "Hi Mrs. Bernell. Can Missy come out and play?" "Hi Amy. I'll see if I can" – just then Missy flew past her and tagged Amy on the arm and said, "You're it!" Jennifer closed the door and went back inside.

After a while the girls decided to play hide and seek. Amy covered her eyes up against a tree in the back yard, while Missy darted around to the front of the house. She sensed a shift in the atmosphere that she didn't understand and couldn't explain. It just made her a little uncomfortable, but she didn't see anything, so she ignored it. The reason for that discomfort was standing near the gate, unseen. Dagon's plan was moving forward. Unnoticed, he opened the back door of Reece's dark gray luxury sedan just as Missy was coming around the corner. She saw that the car door was open, which she thought was a little strange. She didn't see Reece around. *I bet that would make a good hiding spot,* she thought. She climbed into the back, shut the door, and hid under a blanket on the floor. Her eyelids began to feel heavy, and before long she was asleep.

Reece walked out the front door to go to work. He got into his car and started it up without noticing the stowaway just behind him. He roared through the gates and onto the street, waking up Missy. She could tell that the car was moving, but didn't know if she should come out of hiding. Reece took out his cell phone, dialed a number and put it up to his ear. "Gunner – I'm on my way." Missy couldn't hear the other side of the conversation. "Everything ready?" Another pause. "I'll handle it when I get there."

Back at the house, Amy was looking everywhere she could think of, to no avail. *Missy must have found a super good hiding spot,* she thought to herself. "Okay Missy, you can come out now. You win!" No reply. "Missy!" She ran to the other side of the house. "Missy! You won. Come out!" Amy was getting more and more upset, thinking Missy had bailed on her, so she fumed, "Fine! I'll just go home." Then she jumped on her bike and took off.

The Recipient

In the back of the car, Missy heard the phone conversation, but didn't know what to make of it. She didn't know Reece very well. She was a little scared of him. She was worried that he might be mad if he knew that she heard that phone call. The further they got from home, the more scared she became. *Maybe I should stay hidden. He might get mad if he has to turn around to take me home.* She knew something was wrong, and instinctively decided to stay hidden. Reece finally arrived at his warehouse and went inside.

Missy didn't know what to do. She finally got the nerve up to peek out the window. She had never been to this part of the city. She felt a sudden, overwhelming curiosity to know what was going on inside the warehouse Reece had just gone into. Dagon was hovering close by, and whispered to her, *I have to know what's in there.* Missy said under her breath, "I have to know what's in there." Curiosity got the best of her, so she got out of the car and gingerly opened the door to the warehouse. She peeked in but didn't see anyone. Summoning up more courage, she snuck in to get a glimpse into the back part of the warehouse. She didn't notice the security camera overhead, but what she saw made her heart start pounding - in a dimly lit area there was a man tied to a chair, with another man playing solitaire on a card table nearby. She knew she had to get out of there, and got ready to bolt for the front door, but just then she heard the sound of a door opening not too far away from her. She tucked back into a crevice, making herself as small as possible. It was Reece, heading toward the back of the dimly-lit warehouse. He pulled a black automatic pistol out of his holster and without a word shot the man in the chest twice. Missy's jaw dropped open and her eyes got as wide as saucers. She covered her mouth with her hands so she wouldn't scream. She felt like her feet were glued to the floor. Reece said to Gunner, "Help me move him." Gunner nodded and jumped up to help. While they were occupied, Missy realized it was her chance to escape. Her breathing had slowed down a little, and her legs finally obeyed her command to move. She was able to sneak out the door and close it quietly. Now what? Maybe she should find another way home. Maybe she should run and try to get as far away from Reece as possible. Maybe she should find a phone and call mom. Maybe she would be able to make it home the same way she got there. She knew there wasn't much time, so she got back into the back seat of the car. She heard the front door of the warehouse slam, so she dove under the blanket and prayed that God would make her invisible.

Reece got into the car and put his right arm into the back seat so he could back the car up, his fingers touching the blanket Missy was hiding under. She could feel his hand. She held her breath. She had never been more terrified. She was afraid he would feel her heart pounding. Reece finally brought his hand back to the front, as Missy breathed a sigh of relief. When they pulled into the driveway, Reece got out of the car and went inside, but Missy stayed in place for what seemed like hours. She finally got up the courage to sneak out of the car and went back to her room. She sat on her bed and stared at the wall, almost catatonic, unable to erase the image she had just seen from her mind. *Do I tell mom? What if he hurts her? What if he hurts me? Should I run away?*

Watching this whole scenario play out, Dagon couldn't help feeling a little smug. *All according to the plan*, He thought.

The Recipient

Chapter eight

Dream Team

Bear sat in his truck with a look of amazement on his face after his second meeting with Dan and Karen about their new bay window. They decided to work with him for the project – he was glad about that, but he was blindsided by what happened next. When he first walked in and started chit-chatting with them, something felt different. Dan looked different – so much so that Bear mentioned it, and that's all Karen needed. She told him about the change that came over Dan just a couple days ago. It was like a light went on, and after three years of soul-crushing grief, she finally had her husband back. It wasn't that Dan no longer missed his son, but the all-consuming torment had gone, and a peculiar sense of peace had settled over him. He even bought Karen a dozen red roses, which were in a vase on the mantel.

How does this work? Bear asked himself after mulling over everything that happened. After starting his truck he heard it making a noise he hadn't heard before. He got out and listened to the engine. It didn't sound good. *It's always something...* He turned on Sir Patrick to take his mind off stuff like this. He would deal with it later.

Sir Patrick was on a roll *...It's the one-year anniversary of our show, and I have you guys to thank for its success! We have cake on our website. Cake for everyone. Cake is good. We're up to a hundred thousand subscribers! You guys rock! No more talk about* *chemtrails today; I think we've exhausted that topic! Exhaust. I made a pun! Anyway, I did some research on the Georgia Guidestones, and I have one question: WHAT WERE THESE GUYS THINKING?...*

Sunlight streamed into the conference room near Zavan's office overlooking downtown. The whole floor was buzzing with dozens of twenty and thirty-something's milling around. Everyone seemed upbeat. Ten of them were seated at the mahogany conference table with a white board at one side of the room and a large flat screen monitor at the other end. Zavan was standing near the monitor, calling their attention to the onscreen graphic, which looked like a map of the city divided into color-coded sectors. Zavan began, "This gives us a breakdown of the sectors according to the level of influence we have. As you can see, there is an unusually high level of rebel activity here, here, and here," as he was pointing to different zones on the map. One of the celestials around the table asked, "In regard to re-taking territory, have we figured out how to exploit their weaknesses?" Zavan thought for a second and responded, "One of their greatest vulnerabilities is communication, because they don't trust each other." The young one continued, "Given their haphazard communication style, what if we launched an attack on one of their strongholds without orders? You know – just take initiative." Zavan understood where he was coming from. He had been there – zealous and feeling invincible. "What I can tell you from experience, is that we have to have a healthy respect for them. If you go out there unprepared, or take them lightly, you can get into trouble. When Lucifer committed treason, the creator didn't take away his power or authority. Anyway, back to the topic at hand – the resistance *here* is off the charts. We've picked up chatter in this area about the portal to be opened up." As soon as the word 'portal' escaped his lips, the room went completely silent. This was a big deal, and they all wanted more details. At that moment the door opened and Kiandra caught Zavan's attention and motioned to him that they needed to talk. Zavan said to the group, "Let's take a break."

As they were walking through the hall, Kiandra told Zavan, "Dagon found out about the portal. It's hard to keep such a thing a secret when he has such an extensive network." Zavan asked, "How much does he know?" Kiandra replied, "We're not sure. If he found out about the recipient -" Zavan interjected, "He'll stop at nothing." He thought for a moment, "Does this change the timetable?" Kiandra said, "That depends. Is McQuade ready?" Zavan replied, "In my opinion, he is not. I think he needs more time. But I hope I'm wrong. I'll get to work on the preparations."

Several days later, at three a.m. in the Bernell mansion, a child's scream cut through the air. Missy was in bed, terrified and screaming. Jennifer rushed down the hall, threw the door open, and took Missy in her arms. "It's okay, honey, I'm here. It's okay now." Jennifer rocked her back and forth gently like she used to when Missy was a baby. Missy was beginning to settle down, but was still crying. When she was finally able to get her voice under control, she managed to get the words out, "Why don't they stop?" Jennifer looked into Missy's tear-filled eyes, agonized as only a mother can be at watching her child suffer. These nightmares had been going on for several days. Every night she would wake up screaming. Jennifer told her, "I'll sit with you until you fall asleep." Fifteen minutes later, Missy's rhythmic breathing told her that it was okay to go back to bed. Reece came down the hall to check on them as Jennifer was going into the hall, "Any idea why this is happening?" She just looked at him sadly and shrugged her shoulders. He put his arm around her and walked her back to the master bedroom.

The next morning at breakfast, Reece was already gone, and Missy was ignoring a bowl of granola. She just stared out the window. Jennifer asked, "Aren't you hungry?" Missy just shook her head no. Jennifer tried to get her to talk again, "What's wrong honey? You haven't been yourself lately." Nothing. Jennifer continued, "Maybe I should take you to see the doctor." Without looking at her mom, she just shook her head no. "You know what I'd like?" Jennifer said, "I would like to hear you play violin. Would you do that for me? You know it always makes you feel better." Missy thought for a moment, and said, "I guess so." Jennifer gave her a big hug and said, "I love you so much." Wondering if she should push it any further, she asked, "Do you remember anything about the nightmares you've been having?" Missy told her, "I only remember bits and pieces. I think someone's chasing me. And trying to kill me." Trying to be reassuring, Jennifer said, "But it's just a dream, honey."

June 3rd, 1890

A sunny day by the river – the perfect setting for a June wedding. To the casual observer it looked like a perfectly normal, albeit small, wedding: a bride, a groom, the best man and maid of honor, and the minister. The bride was glowing, as many brides do, but the groom also seemed to be glowing. Their love for each other, and the joy that radiated from them was palpable.

Zavan watched closely; he knew something important was happening. The minister spoke, "Do you, Mac McQuade, take Olive Towner to be your lawfully wedded wife?" Mac announced, "I do." The minister asked Olive, "Do you, Olive Towner, take Mac McQuade to be your lawfully wedded husband?" Her eyes sparkled as she said, "Of course I do!" The minister continued, "Then I have the honor of pronouncing you husband and wife: Mr. and Mrs. Mac McQuade! The world will never be the same!"

The minister was just adding his personal touch of humor to the ceremony, but he had no way of knowing that he was, in fact, prophesying – speaking the future into existence.

Bear was in the waiting room at a mechanic's shop, hoping the news wasn't going to be too bad. Just then he glanced over at the gas pumps and saw Marley Aiden, the high school wrestling coach, and walked over to say hi. The coach saw him coming, "Hey Bear, how you doin'?" Bear said, "I'm better than I deserve!" The coach laughed. Bear continued, "You guys are on a roll this year!" Coach Aiden said, "We've had a good season so far!" After a short pause, he asked Bear, "You know, that assistant coach position is still open. Have you thought about my offer?" Bear's smile disappeared. He sighed and said, "You know I appreciate the offer, but I just don't think it would work out well." The two men exchanged some more pleasantries, then Bear saw the mechanic coming out of the work area. Bear excused himself to go talk to the mechanic. After a few minutes of conversation, Bear got into his truck and grumbled under his breath, "Why would I expect anything different?" He recognized that his attitude was sinking fast. He rolled his eyes and said, "Okay, sorry. I'll work on it." Bear had never been comfortable sinking to his knees, folding his hands and using King James English to communicate with God. It just felt too restrictive... too formal. He wanted to be okay with God, but he didn't want to get *too* close. He didn't want it to get weird. There's no telling what God might ask someone to do.

The Recipient

Late afternoon found Bear and Ty riding horses on the
trail near the ranch. Bear was careful not to run Dusty
on pavement because of his hoof, but he did let him
gallop a little on the trails. Ambling through the trees on
horseback was exhilarating for Bear. He was not just
watching nature, but he felt like he was part of it – the
trees, the squirrels… Bear turned to look at Ty, who was
looking at his cell phone. Bear couldn't help himself,
"Isn't it illegal to text while riding horse? If it's not it
should be. Look around you. Don't you want to soak this
in?" Ty responded, "I'm not texting." Bear waited for an
explanation, which did not come. Ty was not himself
today. He seemed a little morose, even for a teenager.
Bear tried again to draw him out. "Learning anything
worthwhile in that psych class?" All he got in response
was, "Not really." Maybe Ty just needed a little space.

---

*Bear was walking in the dark, next to an old building
that looked abandoned. There was someone walking
with him who he didn't recognize, but it didn't seem
abnormal. He was about the same height; a little
younger, no, maybe a little older… it was hard to tell.
There seemed to be an unspoken knowledge between
them that they were supposed to be there. They were
walking toward a large overhead garage door. As they
got closer, he could see a pair of red eyes leering at
them out of the darkness, but it didn't seem like a
problem, though. Bear felt like he was drawing energy
from his new companion. They heard a scream coming*

from inside the building, and could see a little girl running as if her life depended on it, being chased by someone, or something - it appeared human-like, but at the same time, not human. Bear instinctively ran toward the building to help. As he did, the garage door began to close, and he didn't know if he could make it in time. He had to go for it – he lunged at the opening like he was sliding into home plate, just barely making it before the door closed. He ignored the warehouse full of junk, and followed the commotion, and saw the figure chasing the girl. He ran right at him, not stopping to think what he would do when or if he caught him. No need – whatever it was took off through the back door. Bear just caught a glimpse of his face, and it was definitely not someone you would want to meet in a dark alley – or a dark abandoned warehouse. He looked around for the girl but didn't see her. He never did get a good look at her. Zavan caught up to Bear, and without a word, tossed a little vial of liquid in his direction. He caught it and looked at it, silently questioning his new friend, who just nodded toward the back door. Beat understood what to do, as if instructions were being beamed into his head. Going over to the door, he unscrewed the cap and put a little of the oil on his finger and smeared it on the top and sides of the door frame. It smelled like frankincense. Or maybe bergamot. The room started to light up, slowly, as if the walls were glowing. Then the sky opened up, and a shaft of brilliant light shone through the area right in front of him, like a bright tunnel connecting the earth with the sky. He had seen this before – in those visions.

The Recipient

From behind a pile of old lumber, a pair of youthful eyes silently watched everything.

Bear's eyes opened and he scanned the room; he was in his bed, in his bedroom. There was no warehouse, no sidekick, no bad guy and no little girl. Or so he thought.

The Recipient

The Recipient

Chapter nine

Reluctant Prophet

It had been at least a couple days since that dream. Bear parked his truck a block away from his next appointment to go over the details. He looked at his phone. *It's the Bernell residence… Hmm, Bernell, that name sounds familiar. They want some remodeling done in the lower level - sounds like framing, drywall, electric, paint – run of the mill stuff. Okay, time to get this show on the road.*

Bear drove through the gates into the stately front yard, and thought, *wow, this guy has done alright for himself!* He walked up to the sprawling two story brick and stucco house and rang the doorbell. He turned around to admire the finely manicured yard. A well-dressed young black man opened the door. He had thick glasses on, a pastel shirt and tie, and expensive shoes. He said, "You must be from the remodeling service." Bear responded, "Yup." And extended his hand, to which the man handed him a file and said, "Rob Drescher – follow me. Mr. Bernell wants this project started before he gets back, so time is of the essence." They went downstairs to the area to be worked on, and Rob said, "All the details are in the file. I have to make some phone calls. Go ahead and do your thing. I'll be back shortly." The all-business Rob left, so Bear started paging through the file. "This guy's thorough."

The Recipient

Bear won the bid, and started working on the project the following morning. He needed a T-square from his truck, so he headed for the door when he heard someone coming down the stairs. He rounded the corner and came face to face with – he couldn't believe it – Jennifer! They stared at each other for a few seconds, neither one knowing what to say. Suddenly Jennifer slapped Bear across the face. "I probably had that coming." Bear mumbled. He had developed a communication style that could only be described as minimalist. Not Jennifer, though. If something came to her mind, it usually shot out her mouth. "That's all you have to say? After ten years?" He knew he had to say something, but he was on her turf now. "Has it really been ten years?" Maybe that wasn't the right thing to say. "So you're Jennifer... Bernell now?" Jennifer just shook her head. "Out of all the remodelers in the city, Rob picked you." She thought for a moment and before she walked away she said, "You know what? It's a big house. We don't need to see each other." When she was out of sight, Bear let out a big sigh. *What are the odds? I should have bid higher.*

Soon Bear was back to it. He had been hearing sounds coming from a nearby room, but he hadn't paid any attention to it. He heard footsteps from down the hall coming toward him, so he turned around, and saw him. Bear's heart skipped a beat, and he felt his mouth get dry. Reece Bernell. Yes, THAT Reece Bernell. The same Reece Bernell who was driving the car that rammed into him and kept him out of the state tournament all those years ago. Bear's thoughts went a mile a minute.

The Recipient

How did I not remember that name? Does he remember who I am? Does he remember what he did to me? Why did he end up rich while I'm a handyman? How did he end up with Jennifer? Does he know about us? How could he? He doesn't even remember me.

This flood of thoughts came in a fraction of a second. Reece held out his hand, "Reece Bernell." "I'm Bear McQuade." He said guardedly. As he took Reece's hand, the image of a hooded cobra ready to strike came to Bear's mind. Again, Bear was taken aback, but after all this he managed to collect himself. "You have a beautiful home." Reece casually responded, "Haven't been here long – I thought I'd make a few changes. Why don't I show you around?" Bear just replied, "Lead the way." First Reece showed him the workout room, complete with a full wall of mirrors, a dumbbell rack, punching bag, and mat in the center. Bear was visibly impressed. Reece didn't say anything, but seemed interested in his reaction. Reece took him to his den next to show off his weapons collection. The situation reminded Bear of a James Bond movie – Reece seemed like a Bond villain. More thoughts. More questions.

I can do this. I've never walked away from a job, and I'm not going to start now. I'll just keep my mouth shut. Maybe he's just an ordinary, decent guy, and I should give him a chance. And maybe I'll win the lottery seven times in a row. I know, I know. Forgive. Why didn't I just walk away? I don't need this.

Finally Bear said, "So you're a collector? These look old." "And very valuable." Reece replied without any concern about appearing to act the part of the self-absorbed rich snob. "Have you ever done high-end home offices?" Without hesitation, Bear shot back, "Oh yeah – home offices, rec room, panic rooms..." Bear looked at his watch, "I better get back to work"

As completely unprepared for this situation as Bear felt, having unpleasant history with both parties, he thought, *at least it couldn't get any more complicated. Hopefully. Did Jennifer tell her husband about me? Should I assume he knows we have history? This could get really awkward. Maybe I should just bolt for the door. I don't like drama.*

Toward the end of the day Bear was in the living room talking to Reece, updating him about the status of the project. Reece didn't seem particularly interested, but Bear had done this long enough to know that communication was a big part of the job. He didn't see that Jennifer was around the corner in the living room. Missy came out of her room to see what was going on. As she came down the stairs, she saw Bear and stopped dead in her tracks. Her jaw dropped open, then she broke into a run right toward him. She launched herself off the leather hassock and into Bear's arms and wrapped her arms around his neck and said, "I knew you'd come! I saw you chase the bad guy away! Oh! I made something for you!" As she jumped down, Bear looked at Reece, then Jennifer who had come over to see what in the world was going on. They were both staring at him. No one knew what to say. Missy ran to a drawer and pulled out a silver five-pointed star she had made out of aluminum foil and cardboard, and slapped it on Bear's chest. "Thank you for rescuing me. You're the dream sheriff!"

Bear had a look of bewilderment on his face as he looked again from Reece to Jennifer. He thought back to that dream from a few days ago. *That was **my** dream. She was describing **my** dream! That can't happen! But I saw a little girl… What in the world is going on?* As Bear was struggling with his thoughts, Jennifer, who was looking quite uncomfortable with the situation, said to Missy, "Sweetie, can you explain what you mean? Do you know Mr. McQuade?" Missy responded matter-of-factly, as if this type of thing happens all the time, "We met in my dream – or really it was a nightmare. Well, we didn't actually meet, but I saw him. He chased away the monster." Bear figured he better not let on that he knew what she was talking about, so he piped up, "So you had a dream about someone who looked like me?" She protested, "No, it was you, don't you remember? And the other man. My nightmares stopped after that." There was an awkward pause. Jennifer and Reece both looked at Bear, expecting some kind of explanation. Bear said, "I - I've been told I have the kind of face that makes people think they know me…" He was grasping at straws. "In their dreams?" asked Reece. "Well," said Bear, turning back to this sweet little girl in front of him who he had never seen before (at least not in real life), "It's Missy, right?" She nodded as she looked up at him with adoration, which Jennifer picked up on. "When you get older, your brain gets filled up with a bunch of stuff, and when it gets too full, sometimes it has to get rid of some older memories to make room for the new ones. So maybe I was there but I just don't remember it."

The Recipient

Quick thinking. That seemed to satisfy her. He wasn't so sure about the Bernells, though. It seemed anticlimactic, but they had to do a little more shop talk to wrap things up for the day. It might have been his imagination, but it seemed like Jennifer especially was looking at him differently – she had cooled off, and seemed more suspicious than angry.

Her ex shows up out of the blue to work in her house, which is already pretty intrusive, then becomes a hero to her daughter by rescuing her from a monster in a dream, which she apparently thinks is real because her nightmares stopped... What could she possibly be suspicious about?

I didn't ask for this.

Bear got into his truck and shut the door. He didn't even know how to begin to process everything. Was everything that happened some kind of bizarre setup? He glanced around for hidden cameras, then felt a little foolish. No one was watching.

But there was someone watching. Zavan began to write in his journal:

The subject doesn't know he's been chosen to play an important role. That may change soon. I believe his eyes are opening. These puzzle pieces all have to fit together perfectly. He still has a choice, but the decision has been made not to give him the whole picture at this point, or he would pull out his litany of excuses. I've been with him long enough so I know what they are: 'I have no training, I don't have the right background for this, etc. etc.' I guess that's what makes this all the more exciting.

The Recipient

He wouldn't understand yet, but in this realm, natural talent and skills are more of a liability. He has to learn the trust thing.

Bear's phone buzzed, so he picked it up and looked at it. It was a text from Ty that said, 'Don't forget I'm wrestling tonight.'

Bear sent back, 'Wouldn't miss it.'

Bear arrived a little late, so he hustled into the gymnasium to a scene he was all too familiar with – mats on the floor, teams lined up on each side, cheerleaders whipping the crowd into a frenzy... he saw Ty on the mat with his opponent. He glanced at the scoreboard – Ty was down by two points, and was on his stomach, with his arm was behind his back. The referee blew his whistle and said, "Illegal hold: one point penalty." He explained to the other wrestler that you can't bend the other guy's arm behind his back more than 45 degrees toward the shoulder blade or it could break or dislocate his shoulder.

Bear glanced at coach Aiden, who nodded at him. The referee noticed a little blood under the other wrestler's nose, pointed at it, and signaled to start the injury clock. Rubbing his shoulder, Ty walked to the edge of the mat where Bear was standing. Out of breath, he said, "Glad you made it. Too bad I'm losing." Bear knew he needed to break him out of whatever funk he was in, so he said,

"Ty, look at me," in a tone of voice that conveyed some urgency. Ty focused on Bear, wondering what was coming next. "What's going on with you? Where is your head?" Ty looked down kicked a piece of dirt off the mat. "I don't know if this is a good time." Bear shot back, "Whatever it is, it's throwing you off your game. Why don't you get it off your chest?" Ty looked up and said, "I had a dream – I saw you lying in a coffin. It was weird because you were wearing stone-washed jeans and a Members Only jacket. Then another you walked up behind me, so I looked at the other you, then I woke up." Bear said, "So you think it means something." Ty responded, "It sounds stupid when I say it, but I was afraid you're going to die." Bear took a deep breath. The other wrestler was getting patched up, so they didn't have much time left. "Everybody dies – I don't plan on that being anytime soon, though." That didn't seem to help. Bear added, "Sometimes a dream that seems ominous can actually mean something good – you just have to dig a little deeper. Maybe it's a warning – something you need to pray against." Bear could see Ty's countenance change, like some heavy burden lifted off him. "So that's taken care of – can we focus on the match?" Ty understood that his lack of focus was causing him to lose – not his opponent. So Bear continued, "Good, now I want to see side to side movement, touch and go. When you feel him push, hit the over and under throw. But remember... if you want it to work, you have to *commit* to it."

The match resumed, and Ty circled his opponent with a new confidence and focus. He did his setup just like Bear had told him, then when he felt his opponent push, he hit it! It was a textbook throw – Ty took his opponent right to his back and pinned him. When they were back at the center of the mat, they shook hands, the referee raised Ty's hand. He looked over at Bear, who gave him the thumbs up, then he ran back to his teammates who made the traditional high-five tunnel for him at the edge of the mat.

I knew he could do it.

As Bear was driving home, he couldn't get Jennifer out of his head. It wasn't a romantic thing – that ship sailed a long time ago – her face just kept appearing in his mind. Thinking about Jennifer brought up too many unpleasant memories. Too much guilt. Dredging up that part of his history meant that he would have to confront himself and face the ghosts of his past, which felt like death itself.

Why can't I get her out of my mind? I let go of her a long time ago… Maybe I'm supposed to pray for her. That wasn't exactly on my to-do list… Okay, you win. Here goes…

Bear didn't see much sense arguing with the man upstairs. Funny thing about God – he thinks he's God.

June 3rd, 1890

Mac was exuberant, and strong – he picked up his new bride, Olive, and swung her around. As they were kissing, the minister piped up, "I hate to interrupt you two, but... are you ready?" Mac answered, "Chompin' at the bit!" The next part of the ceremony was quite unusual, but they both insisted that it be done this way. Mac, Olive, the minister and the best man waded out into the river about waist deep. The water was colder than they expected, but they didn't care. As Mac and Olive held hands, the two men lowered them into the water until they were completely covered. The maid of honor began reading the vow they had crafted together:

"We consecrate our union and future generations to the destruction of the kingdom of darkness."

Zavan felt a tingle go up his spine as he heard those words. Just after the two were lifted up out of the water, a lightning bolt hit a pine tree just across the river, followed by a loud peal of thunder. They were all stunned – they knew it was a sign.

The Recipient

Chapter 10

Suspicion

Jennifer sat on the barstool at the edge of the kitchen sipping a mimosa and scrolling through her phone, as Reece, Gunner and Rob walked up the stairs toward the front door. She noticed that they lowered their voices as they were coming up the stairs, as if some topics were not for everyone's ears. Reece had never told her much about his associates, so she tried to fill in the details. Gunner was a bald, stocky white guy whose eyes darted around a lot. He looked like he was trying out for the role of a hitman in a movie. She certainly wouldn't be comfortable being alone with him. Rob was a different story: just shy of six feet tall, black, athletic-looking, she couldn't really place his accent. It wasn't exactly Midwestern, but maybe Boston? She couldn't get a read on him. He didn't make her feel uncomfortable, but something felt out of place.

She got up and went to the master bedroom, and into her closet to look for that pair of high heels that seemed to have vanished. She noticed a pair of Reece's shoes that were pushed back against the closet wall, and something made her take notice. Reece was usually fastidious, but these shoes had something on them. She brought them into the light to get a better look. It was subtle, but she could see dark brown flecks on one side. She didn't want to believe it was blood. It could just be grease. It could be anything. She put the shoes back where she found them and tried to push the thought out of her mind. It didn't work. She walked over to the window, where she saw Reece and his associates talking by his car. Gunner bent over to reach for something inside the car, and she saw it – he had a holster with a semi-automatic pistol on his belt. She quickly ducked back out of their line of sight. It would be easier if she hadn't seen that. Now she had to start asking herself some pointed questions. She had always felt there was a wall between Reece and her, an impenetrable barrier. There was also an unspoken rule that it was never to be talked about. The no-talk rule. *What does my husband do for a living? Why do his associates need to carry weapons?* And finally, the big one: *Who the hell did I marry?*

Kiandra and Zavan were walking down the hall in their office complex that was buzzing with activity: celestials conferring with one another, watching computer screens, drinking coffee... they came to a security door, and Kiandra put her palm on a scanner, then punched a code into the keypad. The heavy door opened in front of them, and they walked into a small, dimly lit room. Kiandra entered some information into a keyboard, and a three-dimensional hologram of Reece Bernell appeared in front of them, rotating slowly. Zavan sighed and asked, "How does someone's heart get that hard? You'd think I'd be used to it by now." Kiandra replied, "The heart just wants what it wants. That's the mystery of iniquity. I'll never understand it either." Zavan punched in some numbers on the keyboard, and the image of Reece disappeared, and a hologram of Dagon appeared in front of them. "What would my next move be if I were Dagon?" Zavan whispered.

Bear saw the flashing lights in his rear-view mirror, so he pulled over so the police car could pass him. To his surprise, he was the one being pulled over. He looked in his side mirror to see a state trooper walking toward him, but couldn't see his face. Bear rolled down his window to look in the face of the 'monster' he had chased away in Missy's dream. Dagon. It felt like icy fingers wrapping around his heart. Bear wasn't sure what to do. His thoughts started racing:

If this is a dream, I can do anything and it won't matter. I can't get hurt in a dream, right? What if this isn't a dream? What is he? Wait – in a dream you never think about how you got into a situation. Where was I before this?

"License and registration please." Came the voice behind the sunglasses. Facing forward and gripping the steering wheel, Bear asked in a controlled voice, "What do you want?" The trooper responded, "I want to help you." Bear didn't say anything. He sat still as a statue. He wasn't paralyzed, but felt almost as if he was not in complete control of his body. It was like a hypnotic trance. The man continued, "Self-preservation is a powerful motivating force."

The Recipient

Whether this is a dream or not, why would I sit and listen to riddles from a phantom?

He worked up the courage to say, "Is there something I can do for you, officer?" The man ripped off his sunglasses, revealing cold, penetrating eyes, and hissed, "Leave her alone. Don't talk to her, don't pray for her, don't even think about her." Bear wasn't sure how to respond, but he knew playing dumb was not an option. This man, this creature, whatever it was, knew about his situation, and did not want to be trifled with. Still facing forward, Bear asked, "Or what?" Dagon continued, "I'll do what I do best. Do not underestimate me."

Dagon walked back to his car, pulled a U-turn and sped away. Bear shook his head as if snapping out of the trance, then put his truck in gear and squealed his tires while doing a U-turn. He floored it, heading up the hill the police car disappeared behind. At the top of the hill, there were no cars to be seen. He had disappeared into thin air. He grabbed a marker from the middle console of his truck and hurriedly drew a skull on the inside of his left forearm.

When Bear was back home later on that evening, he felt something strange in the house, but he couldn't put his finger on it. All of the sudden, one of the kitchen cabinet doors flew open by itself. Then a picture fell off the wall in the living room. Bear's eyes darted around the room, then he said out loud, "Is that all you got?" He looked at his left arm and saw that the drawing of skull was still there. That meant his experience wasn't a dream, or that he was still in it. He sat down in his favorite chair and opened up his Bible and laptop, and a notepad, and spent a few minutes going through some pages, highlighting a few passages, and writing some notes.

Jennifer was in the kitchen, putting away some silverware from the dishwasher. In her current state of mind, the music from the built-in speakers was more irritating than soothing, so she gave the command to kill the music. Now there was silence, and she was alone with her thoughts, which were not at all subtle. They were ganging up on her.

What does Reece know? I can't stand the tension in the house. I've got to get out of here.

Just then Reece's car pulled in the driveway, which didn't help Jennifer calm down. She put a serving spoon away in the drawer as Reece came in the front door. As he walked to the kitchen, Jennifer felt a tightness in her chest. She felt like running. Reece seemed oblivious to her mood as he greeted her.

Is he going to bring it up? How much does he know?

He said, "You seem to be getting along well with the handyman." She could sense his disdain for Bear, referring to him as 'the handyman'. She knew where this conversation was headed. It was time to deflect and distract. "I like the fact that he respects our house. He seems like he knows what he's doing." Reece wasn't taking the bait. "I'm not talking about his competence. You seem to have a … connection with him."

Spin and dance. Shuck and jive. I'm a woman. I can talk rings around him.

"He seems like a decent guy. Missy sure has taken a shine to him." Reece immediately responded, "I've noticed that, too."

Wrong answer. Nothing like reminding a man that his stepdaughter likes another man better than she likes him. Try again.

"You have to admit this is an unusual situation – you know, that dream." She put another plate away, looking for any reason to avoid eye contact. "He's in the dark as much as we are." Reece didn't miss a beat, "So you've talked to him about it?" A high-octane ping went right through her, like when you watch your child skin her knee, and you can feel it.

I really blew it that time. Why did I say that? I just keep digging myself deeper into this hole. He's setting a trap for me.

"Well, I talked to him about it when I ran into him downstairs. I just wanted to find out his story." Reece continued to press in. "And what is his story?" As Jennifer put a mixing bowl in the cupboard, she replied, "Like I said, he doesn't know any more than we do. I think we can chalk it up to a little girl's overactive dream life. You know how emotional girls can be." The tension hadn't abated. His eyes revealed nothing, like a poker player. Nothing she said had worked so far to decrease his suspicions. "Granted." He went on, "but you two almost seem like old friends."

He said it. He must know something. If I tell him the truth… no, it's too late for that. I've got to hold on. I've got one last shot.

There's a reason Jennifer used to be a model. She had a killer smile that could melt any man's heart. It had kept her out of trouble, and a few times had gotten her into trouble. But this situation was different. She was scared, and really didn't know what he would do. She took a deep breath, turned to face him and flashed that million-dollar smile, "Reece, you have absolutely nothing to worry about. He just seems to have a quality that puts people at ease." Reece didn't answer, but walked toward her, showing no emotion whatsoever. She was afraid he would hear her heart about to beat out of her chest. She froze. There was nothing else she could do. She couldn't fight him. If she ran, he would catch her. And what about Missy? *God, help me. Help us.* He put his hand on her shoulder and kissed the back of her neck, then walked away. Jennifer looked down at her hands, which were shaking. She felt like she was going to pass out.

What just happened? Is this all just in my head? Am I going crazy? Why would I think my husband wants to kill me?

The Recipient

Bear was doing calculations on a piece of paper in the lower level of the mansion, making preparations for a new wall, when he heard violin music coming from the family room. It commanded his attention. It got down deep inside of him and stirred up something, like opening a door to a room that had been sealed for a long time. He put down his pencil and went to the doorway of the family room and watched as Missy practiced. The music seemed to wrap around him and seep into him. In his mind's eye he saw a vision of what looked like a tornado made of light. The light seemed to be made up of 'strands' that slowly swirled around each other. Missy turned her head and noticed him. "Bear?" He heard it again. "Bear?" Missy's voice snapped him out of his trance. "Don't you like it?" Bear stammered back, "Oh, uh… no, I mean yes. I like it a lot. You're really good. I can feel it when you play." Bear said as he pointed to his chest. He heard the entry door upstairs slam as Reece and his associates came into the house. Just then Jennifer walked into the room. She didn't look angry; she looked scared. She grabbed him by the arm and took him back to the area he had been working in, slipped a note into his hand and whispered, "Meet me here." She went back into the family room and said to Missy, "Don't stop, honey, it sounds great!" Bear heard Reece coming, so he quickly put the note in his pocket and got back to work. Reece and Rob walked by the area as he heard Reece say in a low voice, "We'll go through the rest of it at the lake house." Bear and Rob looked at each other for about two seconds, as if sizing each other up.

Later on, Reece approached Bear with his workout gear on. "So, Bear, have you ever done mixed martial arts?" Bear replied, "No, believe it or not I like my face just the way it is." Not wanting to drop it, Reece asked, "What do you say we do a little sparring?" Bear couldn't help wondering why he was asking, and where this was going. "I think I better decline. I imagine your associate would give you more of a challenge. Besides, I have a lot of work to do here." Reece said," I think you're being modest. Gunner is good, but he's a little predictable. Here's what I'll do – I'll tack on fifty percent to your estimate." Bear's eyebrows shot up. *Fifty percent!* "That does make it more tempting... Okay, you got yourself a sparring partner."

Soon they were both suited up, complete with MMA gloves, protective belts, and headgear. Without a word, they walked to the center of the mat and squared off. Bear did a traditional bow, and Reece showed a hint of a smile and did the same. Reece took his fighting stance and moved toward Bear, who noticed how smoothly Reece was moving, as if he had been practicing this for a long time, and he felt a tinge of concern. Reece took a couple jabs towards Bear's head, which he deflected. Suddenly Reece faked a jab and came around with a hard right hook, followed by a left cross, sending Bear to the mat, literally seeing stars, or spots of light. Bear sensed there was more going on than a simple sparring match. He struggled to his feet. Reece closed in and caught Bear with a right, but he was able to trap Reece's arm and get him in a clinch, then dove in for a takedown. He ended up on top of Reece, slapped the mat and jumped back to his feet. Reece got back up with a very determined look on his face. Someone could get hurt, but it was too late to back out. Reece came toward him with the look of a lion attacking its prey. Bear didn't even remember what happened next, except that it hurt, and he went down. Reece followed him to the mat and raised his fist to strike... They caught eyes for a moment, then Bear slapped the mat with his hand. That meant it was over, and Reece won. But he didn't move. Reece seemed to be contemplating whether or not to finish him off.

Finally, Reece got up, and Bear breathed a sigh of relief. Without a word, Reece walked out of the room and returned drinking a bottle of water, and offered an ice pack to Bear, who sat down against the wall and put it on the left side of his face. Finally Bear spoke, "I guess we have different definitions of the word sparring." Reece coolly responded, "I took the opportunity to give you an object lesson. I've learned how to get what I want, and it works for anyone." Bear just looked at him.

What arrogance! This guy thinks he can 'teach me a lesson?!' Is this about that dream? Does he think I'm drawing his stepdaughter away from him? Maybe he knows about my history with Jennifer. Was this about Jennifer? Does he know about our past relationship? Was this payback?

Reece continued unapologetically, "Learn what the rules are, then strategically break them." Bear replied somewhat sarcastically, "I'll keep that in mind." Reece kept going, "Do you want to know why I was so confident that you wouldn't be a problem?" Bear said the first thing that came to his mind, "Because you've been practicing Muay Thai for ten years?" Not caring if he sounded a little disrespectful. "Beyond that," he replied, "I could *see* just by the way you move that you can handle yourself, but when I looked into your eyes, there was no fire." Bear's thoughts were now redlining:

Who does this guy think he is? Should I tell him what I think of him? Is the right thing to do to just turn the other cheek? My left one is already pretty sore. This guy needs Jesus. Maybe I should just keep my mouth shut. That's always been a pretty safe bet. You can't get in hot water for something you don't say.

Jennifer was sitting in a booth at an uptown coffee shop, while Missy was playing on her tablet in the kids' area not too far away, using a coloring app. It was a nice, generic coffee shop with a few hipsters glued to their laptops and sipping lattes. She wasn't sure if Bear would come. He had just put the note in his pocket when Reece came in. If he had seen that, who knows what he would have done. Jennifer wasn't even sure if Reece was the jealous type. Even after being married to him for a few months, there were a lot of things she didn't know about him. Maybe that's just the way it is when you marry a rich guy. There are trade-offs. It made her uneasy, though. Even though to an outsider it looked like she married well, she desperately wanted to connect with him on a deeper level. Maybe he didn't go any deeper than that. Or maybe *she* didn't want to dig any deeper. A clandestine meeting with her ex was a big risk, but she felt there was no other option. She needed some answers.

Bear finally arrived, clad in a jean jacket and cowboy hat. She remembered why she fell for him in the first place and was surprised at herself for what she was thinking.

Bear walked up to the table, and Jennifer said, "Thanks for coming". There was an awkward pause, and she continued, "Join me?" He sat across from her, scanning the room with his eyes. He wasn't in the habit of meeting with married women, especially without their husband's knowledge. Missy saw Bear and jumped up and ran to the table, "Hi Bear! Look what I drew!" Bear looked at the tablet and said to her, "That's really good! I like it." Jennifer cut in, "Honey, could you let us talk for a little bit?" She looked back to Bear and smiled, then went back to the kids' area. Bear commented, "Sweet kid... Now what's up with this cloak and dagger stuff?" Jennifer let out a heavy sigh, "Where do I even start?... Okay first, how do you explain that dream?" Bear shifted in his seat, "I - um, I can't." Jennifer continued, "Whatever happened, her nightmares stopped." Bear swallowed hard and said, "She seemed pretty convinced it was me." Jennifer just looked at Bear for a few seconds, and he became visibly uncomfortable. She thought carefully about her next words. Some words build bridges that shouldn't exist, while other times they burn bridges that need to be there. Jennifer took a deep breath and began. "Reece doesn't know – about us. I never told him. This whole thing happened so fast I didn't have time to think." Bear didn't show anything, but he felt somewhat relieved that Reece didn't know. But if he didn't know, he must have picked up on something – some connection they had. What was that 'sparring session' about yesterday? A man doesn't just beat the crap out of his handyman for kicks. Jennifer continued, "I know you well enough to know when you're holding out on me." She cocked her head and looked at him, the way she used to when she wanted more information than he was giving. Bear looked away for a moment, but he knew it was no use. He lowered his voice, "All right, I remember it. It's not the kind of dream you forget. It was about a week ago. It all happened just like she said. I remember chasing away a bad guy and anointing a door with oil. Don't ask me how any of this is possible." Jennifer asked, "Did you see Missy?" Bear responded, "No. Well, yes." He was getting flustered. She opened her eyes wide and stared at him, as if she didn't believe him. Bear continued, "I couldn't see her face." Changing the subject, Bear said, "What's going on with you guys?" Jennifer sighed and said, "I married Reece on the rebound earlier this year. I hardly knew anything about him. He was very charming... and rich." Bear wanted to know, "What does he do, exactly?" She replied, "Import/export, antiquities dealer – that's how he explained it." There was a pause in the conversation, while Bear formulated the question that addressed the elephant in the room. "So... what are we doing here?" Jennifer knew it was time to put up or shut up. If she was really going to bring Bear into this, she would be breaking confidence with her husband. She felt she had no choice. "I've been noticing some things... they were always there, but I just couldn't see them. Or maybe I didn't want to see them. It's almost like I was under a spell, but my eyes are open now and I can't keep pretending everything is okay. It may sound crazy, but I'm afraid my husband is into some bad stuff. I've seen things I can't ignore." Bear, getting a little impatient, said, "You're right – it does sound crazy. Seriously, though, I'm not exactly your favorite person. I don't think I need to remind you about the circumstances of our… breakup. So, I'll ask you again; what does this have to do with me?" Jennifer began to feel vulnerable, and her eyes showed it. Bear hated that – she could use that look to get anything she wanted. Regardless of what happened in the past, she was sincere this time. And scared. "Bear, I prayed for help. I asked for a second chance. Or maybe a third… or twentieth chance. Do you believe in coincidences?" Bear took a breath to answer, but Jennifer continued, "Do you know how long it's been since I prayed? And then out of the blue you showed up." Bear's eyes opened wide; he was visibly perturbed, "And you think I'm the answer to your prayer?! I thought you knew me!" Bear thought for a moment, while Jennifer realized she had pushed him too far. He continued on his diatribe, "Look, if you want a gourmet dinner, you call a chef. If you want your husband arrested, you call the sheriff." Bear stood up to leave, but couldn't hold back one more poignant comment; "And if you want to ruin your life, you call me. I thought you knew that. This conversation is over." Bear stormed out, not even turning around to see Jennifer on the verge of tears, or Missy innocently playing on her tablet. On the way to get into his truck, he didn't notice Rob, one of Reece's goons, watching from his car across the street.

Back at Zavan's office, Kiandra was in the middle of a conversation with Zavan.

Kiandra: "How's our boy progressing?"

Zavan: "He's a tough case – he feels like he's damaged goods. Sometimes I just want to grab him by the shoulders and shake him..."

Zavan made the motions of grabbing somebody by the shoulders and violently shaking him. Kiandra looked at him and covered her mouth to keep from laughing. He knew she wasn't laughing *at* him. She had been in this situation more times than she could count. She was used to human frailty. He was a little irritated, though. He wanted to say, 'Come on – lives are at stake! Souls are at stake!' He knew what she would say. That's the one constant - the one thing that never changes: lives and souls are *always* at stake.

Kiandra: "I've been there. Too many times to count."

Zavan: "This baggage is sapping his strength; it's like slow suicide. For him to accomplish his mission, he has to get beyond this. I'm more than a little concerned about him. If he can't step up..."

Kiandra: "Do you think we should bring someone else in?"

Zavan: "I don't think we have time. I just have to believe he'll come through... If he just knew how high the stakes are. Maybe we need to increase the volume a little. You know – to get through to him."

Kiandra: "Agreed. Also we should go over some of the archives – maybe we've overlooked something."

Zavan nodded in agreement, so Kiandra typed something into the control panel. The lights in the small room dimmed, as a screen came down from the ceiling on the far end of the room. Across the screen it read: Seven months ago.

Reece was sitting at a table in a bar with a number of good-looking people. Some were seated, some milling around, presumably on the prowl for their next date. He took a sip of a martini, as the screen revealed a familiar figure sitting next to him. It became clear from watching that Reece thought he was alone. The stranger was Dagon, and he was watching Reece. Jennifer was sitting alone at the bar. He focused on Reece and said, "Wow. I should buy her a drink." Reece couldn't take his eyes off Jennifer. He repeated, "Wow. I should buy her a drink." Dagon said into the air, "How about now?" Reece stood up and said, "No time like the present." He approached Jennifer with a casual confidence and said, "I need to buy you a drink." Jennifer turned around and smiled and nodded toward an open barstool next to her. "By the way, my name is Reece." More small talk ensued – the usual stuff that goes on in a bar.

Kiandra and Zavan compared notes. They knew better than to underestimate Dagon. He always did his homework. When he had a goal, he studied the people involved. He studied the background of individuals, he learned their habits, their likes and dislikes, their weaknesses... He learned how to bend them to his will, all while never letting them know of his existence. If he ever had to reveal himself, that meant he was desperate. He knew the difference between influence and possession. Influence was just a matter of pushing the right buttons: temptation, fear, ego, deception... nothing was off limits. He knew how to use the carrot *and* the stick. Possession was a different matter entirely. Possession required a great deal of work to create an opening. In some cases, years of planning and work were involved. The old sales adage applied perfectly: How much pressure do you apply to close the deal? Just enough. He also knew it was useless to try to possess someone who was in a relationship with the creator – the seal on them made possession impossible. But influence... as long as they were wearing their earth suit, there was a chance to influence them.

The Recipient

The Recipient

Chapter eleven

Head Games

Bear was sitting at his desk at home, in front of the computer screen, thinking back to when he shook hands with Reece and saw a vision of a hooded cobra.

Was that just my own mind playing tricks on me? Was it the gift? The 'seer' gift? I might as well look it up. I might learn something. It beats watching CSI reruns.

He clicked open a video website and typed in 'cobra'. The search turned up a lot of videos, one of which caught his attention. He clicked on it and watched. It looked like something out of National Geographic, complete with a British-sounding narrator: *The cobra is a dangerous poisonous snake that can grow up to 18 feet. They are found mostly in Asia, and can lift one third of their bodies off the ground while moving forward to attack. To intimidate their prey, they flare out their hoods and emit a bone-chilling hiss that sounds like a dog growling. It's not an empty threat either – the cobra is just as venomous as the Black Mamba. The King Cobra can be temporarily subdued by a snake charmer, but it is achieved by the movement rather than the music. Its natural enemy is the mongoose, which is immune to a certain amount of cobra venom. In a confrontation, the mongoose strategically waits for the cobra to leave an opening, however small, then strikes.*

It had been a productive morning on the Bernell job. Bear was sitting on the back deck, drinking coffee from his thermos. His mind was busy planning the next step of the project, when Reece came around the corner, looking a little more intimidating than usual. In his all-business manner, he said, "Walk with me." Bear got up and followed him into the backyard. Bear looked to his right and saw Jennifer in the living room, watching them. He was too far away to see the concern registering on her face. They headed toward a wood chipper, which was being used by two men to clean up some of the undergrowth on the property. As they got closer, Reece motioned to them to shut off the machine. When it was off, he told them to take a break, so they headed toward the house. Reece, looking at the wood chipper, spoke without looking at Bear, "For some reason I'm fascinated by these machines. Did you know that this one can chew up a log six inches in diameter? Then it becomes mulch – landscaping material." Bear calmly played along, "I've never used one this big." Reece changed the subject, "Do you have a family, Mr. McQuade?" Bear knew when someone was fishing for information that could be used against him. He used his words sparingly. "Used to." Reece continued fishing, "Divorced?" At this point, Bear was more annoyed than intimidated, "Something like that." He refused to give Reece any extra information or reveal his feelings. This job would be over soon. Then he could forget all about this. Either Reece had a sentimental side to him, or he was a sociopath that could read people and imitate emotions. Bear hadn't figured him out yet. "Family is very important to me. Family, marriage... til death do us part; that's the vow we took. I don't believe in divorce."

The Recipient

After thinking for a moment, Bear responded, "A divorce is kind of like an earthquake. Nobody wants it; you don't ask for it; it does a lot of damage, but sometimes it just happens." Reece said nothing, he just looked at the wood chipper and quickly turned it on, then off. Message sent and received.

Bear was driving his truck home, and turned on the radio – his driving companion, Sir Patrick was on: *...next we're going to dig into the connection between the DC swamp and MI6; the unholy alliance between rogue elements of American and British intelligence. The media call us conspiracy nuts, but we know better, don't we, boys and girls?*

Suddenly Bear couldn't hear the voice on the radio – he was witnessing a scene from what looked like the inside of a dark warehouse. Reece was walking toward a man tied to a chair, and pulled out a gun and –

What in the world am I seeing? He just killed him! That's Reece! Is this real?

As Bear's heart rate skyrocketed, The scene changed, and there was a room he didn't recognize. Jennifer was tied up in a chair... Bear's hands were shaking from the adrenaline rush, so he pulled to the side of the road so he wouldn't pass out from hyperventilating. "I have to run this by somebody," he said as he caught his breath. He pulled a U-turn and sped off down the road.

The Recipient

Before long Bear was knocking on the door of a house in a posh neighborhood. As Neal opened the door, Bear walked through and said, "Am I going crazy? Be honest." Without missing a beat, Neal responded, "Yup, next question?" Bear shot back, "I'm serious, man. I'm really think I may be losing it." Neal had gotten used to Bear's 'experiences'. Being more or less agnostic, Neal didn't encourage Bear to pursue these 'visions' *or* tell him it was just overactive neurons. He said, "Are you still getting those…" he waved his fingers and made a humming sound that sounded like a spaceship. Bear sighed and shook his head, "It's hard to explain." Neal went on, "You know, I'm not really into the hidden realm thing. If I can't see it, touch it, drink it or spend it…" They both said together, "it's not real." Bear knew where Neal stood on these things, which is why he confided in him. Neal didn't understand this stuff, but he was intrigued and knew Bear was a straight shooter, and could be trusted. "Oh, it gets better." Bear said, "Jennifer's involved!" Neal rolled his eyes and said, "Sounds like a soup sandwich. Oh boy, I need a drink." He knew this would be a good story. He walked over to his bar and pulled out a glass. "I'd offer you one, but I know what your answer will be." Bear surprised him with, "You know, I think I'll have one tonight." Neal's eyebrows shot up, and he reached for another glass, and poured a little whiskey into it. Bear took the glass and said, "Maybe this will make this whole thing go away." Neal responded, "I've been hopin' that for a long time." Bear asked, "Has it ever worked?" Neal replied without even thinking, "Nope." They clinked their glasses together and took a drink. Bear grimaced after tasting the whiskey, "Now I remember why I don't drink this stuff." Bear went on to tell Neal about the events that had taken place in the last few days, as well as some of his more 'ethereal' experiences. Neal looked a little out of his element as he was taking it all in. "This much I can tell you," Neal said after hearing the whole story, "I've been around the block, and I know the difference between reality and fantasy. I've seen people ruin their lives chasing superstitions and fairy tales because they're so desperate to attach some meaning to their existence. This is different – there's something very real about what's happening to you. I don't understand it, but you'd be a fool to ignore it."

Bear got into his pickup, started it up, and instinctively hit the radio button. Sir Patrick was on a roll.

Hey kids, we're back on the air talking about your destiny. Do you know why you're here? Are you destined to do something great? You're here for a reason, you know. You are not an accident. I happen to believe that everything that's happened to you can be turned around and used for good. Now I know some of you are skeptical – you think there's no rhyme or reason to your life; stuff just happens, and it doesn't mean anything. Well I beg to differ. Some of you are even running away from what you've been called to do...

Bear looked at the radio, feeling confused and irritated, and hit the scan button. The song that came out of the speakers was Highway to Hell, from that heavy metal rock group that was big back in the eighties. Bear's eyes opened a little wider, and he quickly hit the power button to shut it off, almost like the radio was a snake that would bite him if he wasn't quick enough. He let out a heavy sigh and shook his head.

Back in his office, Zavan was watching Bear on his monitor and writing in his journal. *Time is of the essence. We don't have the luxury of waiting around anymore. I'm going to have to give him a push.*

The Recipient

Chapter twelve

Stones of Fire

It's like that old joke about the definition of consciousness: it's that annoying thing that occurs between naps. Bear looked forward to sleep because it gave him a break from having to process everything that was happening. He liked sleep, but not the cryptic dreams – or the nightmares.

Bear found himself back in that dark room, looking at a door that was cracked open just a bit with an extremely bright light shining through it. His instinct was to go back, but this time he decided to move toward the light. Yes, it was a mystery, and that meant he wasn't in control. Now was as good a time as any to admit that control is an illusion. He was acting out in realtime the understanding that life has never been about control, but trust. As he slowly opened the door and stepped over the threshold, the room was so bright it was blinding. As his eyes gradually adjusted to the light, he could see a door on the opposite side of the room that he hadn't noticed before. He was drawn to it, so he cautiously walked over and stepped through into a dark room that looked like a private movie theater, with several overstuffed, burgundy velvet chairs facing a screen that covered the entire wall. Someone wanted him to watch a movie. Would that be wise in such an unfamiliar situation? He felt nothing dangerous or sinister in his gut, only a strange combination of exhilaration and peace, so he picked out a chair, sat down and grabbed a bucket of popcorn that was on the table between the chairs. The screen immediately lit up. The first feature looked like a vintage film from the seventies. The camera panned around a familiar living room scene with a plaid couch near a franklin fireplace, and red tiffany lamp hanging in the corner. It landed on a black and white television with Billy Graham in the middle of a message: "...now is the day of salvation. If you've never given your heart to the Lord..." The camera panned the room again to reveal Bear as a five year old boy watching this man on TV. Bear realized he was watching his life unfold onscreen. He was at a loss for words, completely transfixed. He vaguely remembered the next few minutes as they played out onscreen. The boy ran to the playground and up to the top of the highest slide. He looked up to where he thought heaven must be and whispered, "Okay. You can have me." The camera panned wide to reveal the same man that Bear recognized from that dream he had shared with Missy; he was watching from the edge of the playground. Bear just shook his head. Maybe nothing would ever surprise him again, but he still didn't know who this was, or what he was doing.

He watched a few more scenes from his past: the wrestling matches, the accident... The possibility crept up on him that maybe everything really is connected, and there is a plan. The next scene was that awful day at the hospital. He didn't need or want a video reminding him that his baby died because of his foolish decision. He stood up to leave, but he heard a voice inside his head that said loudly and firmly, "Stay." Wondering where the voice came from, he sat back down, only to find the chair next to him was taken. Bear nearly jumped out of his skin. This was the same guy that was in Bear's dream – the same one watching him during the playground scene. He was wearing blue jeans and a black leather jacket and had his feet up on the hassock. As the man pointed at the screen, Bear heard, "This is my favorite one." The man's lips didn't move, but Bear heard the voice in his head. With too many questions to know which one to ask first, he just sat down and watched. It showed Bear riding a horse on a trail ride. He remembered this one. The horse suddenly bucked and threw him off. The camera angle showed Bear's head traveling right toward a rock. The man next to him showed up onscreen with a shimmery appearance. He stuck out his hand and caught Bear's head before it hit the rock. Bear turned to look at his host with his mouth open... where to start... "You had to know that was me!" the man said with a big smile. "Anyway, let's go." He grabbed Bear's arm, and there was a big flash of light.

This time Bear found himself and his new friend in an incredibly beautiful meadow near a forest, where there were several children playing. One was examining a ruby he had just found, when a huge brown bear came up behind him at the edge of the forest, and... nuzzled him. The boy turned around and laughed, climbed up on its back and they galloped off. There were two girls nearby, making huge bubbles that would turn into various shapes, like temporary statues. The joy in the air was palpable. He had never even imagined anything like this. His attention turned to a group of kids playing with a whole bunch of Beagle puppies. Overhead there were two twenty-somethings hang gliding over a group of kids playing tag. Ten minutes ago, Bear would have had a *million questions, but now, everything just seemed to make sense. Bear just looked at his companion and asked, "Am I dead?" Zavan didn't answer the question; instead he asked, "Do you remember playing frozen tag when you were little?" Bear nodded. Zavan directed Bear's attention to the little boy who was 'frozen', and asked, "Does that remind you of anyone?" Bear knew exactly what he was talking about. Ever since that one mistake: the motorcycle ride – the one decision that cost him everything, he had been frozen. His life was essentially over. He had always believed he didn't deserve a second chance. How do you come back from that? He felt he deserved whatever punishment life dished out. Zavan interrupted his thoughts, "It's time for you to be unfroze." Bear said, "What am I supposed to – "Zavan interrupted him again, "brace yourself." Immediately he heard the voice of a little boy behind him say, "Hi Daddy!"*

As Bear spun around to see who it was, everything went into ultra-slow motion as memories flooded back into his mind: the motorcycle ride, the hospital scene, the little grave marker... Then he looked into the face of a perfect little boy who was smiling at him. This was too much. Bear's knees buckled, and he hit the ground. Smirking, Zavan said, "I told you to brace yourself!" From the ground he stared incredulously at the boy, then at Zavan. He asked, "What's his name?" Zavan said, "Why don't you ask him?"

*This was **the** moment. The moment Bear had been desperately trying to avoid for years. He was now face to face with the life that had been snuffed out because of* *his... foolishness? Ego? Immaturity? Stupidity? Take your pick. There was no avoiding it now. He looked into the eyes of the boy, and didn't see what he expected. No hurt, no disappointment, no anger, no condemnation, only joy. His thoughts were interrupted when the boy said, "You haven't named me yet."*

Years of depression, hopelessness and guilt dissolved in a few seconds. He could feel it leaving as he exhaled. Bear said, "How —" his question was cut short by Zavan, who was practically giddy seeing his charge beginning to enter into his destiny, "That kind of darkness can't exist here. He couldn't hold a grudge even if he wanted to." Just then a little girl called to the boy to come and play. He turned to go, then looked back and said, "I gotta go. Don't forget to name me!" The boy took off running. As he joined his friends, he shouted over his shoulder, "I love you, Daddy!"

At that moment, one of the kids playing tag ran to the boy that was frozen and tagged him. He immediately let out a whoop and joined the others. After watching Bear's reaction, Zavan reached out and touched Bear on the top of his head. The next thing Bear remembered was waking up on his living room floor. Something was different. That nagging sense of emptiness that had dogged him for so long was nowhere to be found. The guilt, the condemnation... gone. It's not that he couldn't remember the past, but it no longer had a grip on him. The future didn't seem so bleak anymore. Maybe he could even hope for something good...

The Recipient

The Recipient

Chapter thirteen

Backlash

April 1900

Ten years had passed for Mac and Olive, and they now
had children – all born under the covenant which they
had pronounced on their wedding day. They hadn't
seen any indications that they were making a dent in
the kingdom of darkness, but they knew that something
was being birthed in the spirit realm. Their part was not
to make something happen, but simply to be faithful.

Olive walked into the parlor where Mac was reading in
his favorite chair, "Mac, have you seen Shannon?" He
looked up at his bride, which is what he still called her,
"I think she's in the barn practicing." Olive went out to
the barn and found Shannon playing her violin, with her
little brother watching and listening. She didn't see her
come in. Olive sat down on a bale of hay and opened up
her journal – a beautifully crafted, leather bound book
and started drawing the scene. She had decided to keep
a journal to help connect her descendants to their
family and their destiny.

Zavan loved listening to Shannon play the violin – there
was a quality to the music that was beyond this
dimension. It strengthened him. Even the farm animals
were more at peace when she played. This little girl was

special, no doubt about it, but was she the one chosen to open the portal?

Mac had her play when one of the cows was having a difficult birth, and both mother and calf pulled through. He told some of the neighbors about it – most of them thought it was just a coincidence, but Mac knew. Unfortunately, Dagon knew also. He knew that this girl was a threat, as was her family. A threat he would have to deal with sooner or later.

Bear was frantically running down a busy city street at night, but nobody was paying attention. Someone or something was after him. He looked over his shoulder, but he didn't see anything. He tried to go faster, but his body wouldn't respond. If felt like he was running through molasses. Dagon materialized about fifty feet behind him in full celestial mode – leathery bat-like wings outstretched, eerily long arms with claws at the ends of his fingers, a pockmarked, ghoulish face... Finally Bear was able to speed up – he took a left into the alley at full tilt, but he found it was a dead end. He stopped to look around. His senses were on full alert - He could smell the dumpster next to him with the distinctive odor of onion peels and coffee grounds, and could clearly see a spider at his chest level working its way up the decaying brick wall.

On a rooftop across the street, Zavan and Kiandra watched helplessly as Dagon stalked Bear. This was especially hard for Zavan, because he was Bear's protector. Neither of them knew why they had been given stand-down orders. Zavan desperately wanted to intervene. "He's doing it again. I can't lose another one!" Kiandra couldn't help seeing the tortured look in his eyes. "No one blames you for what happened. That was a long time ago." She could see that he was contemplating taking unauthorized action. He was passionate and a little unorthodox, but he had never deliberately violated protocol. He clenched his jaw and said, "I blame myself. We were made for action, not deliberation." As he was about to leap off the roof, Kiandra got his attention, "Zavan!" The seriousness of her tone snapped him out of his thought process. She was not in the habit of raising her voice. "There will be a time for that, but it is not now. Stand down!" Zavan knew he had to make a decision. "How can I just do nothing?" Kiandra said, "Obedience is not nothing. If you go rogue, you could ruin everything." Zavan knew she was right, even though it didn't ease the pain of watching his charge suffer.

Back in the alley, Dagon closed in on Bear, who had resigned himself to what he thought might be his fate. "No matter what you do to me, you can't win." Dagon raised his palm toward Bear, and he flew up against the building, unable to escape. "I'm so tired of hearing that." Dagon said as he fastened his hand around Bear's neck. while his hair slowly turned white, Bear struggled against the vicelike grip. Dagon was irritated that his victim wasn't more fearful. He loved fear. He fed on it. "Heroes are overrated." Then he put his face near Bear's left ear and hissed, "You have no idea who you're messing with." Then he launched upward, holding onto Bear, who was struggling to breathe. They went up and up, until the cars looked like toys. Bear instinctively struggled to free himself from the hand that was clamped around his neck, not thinking that if he was able to free himself, he would fall to his death. Dagon stopped ascending and looked into Bear's defiant eyes. "Do you know some people actually want to be martyrs? I love them. It's a win/win." Then he let go, and Bear started falling to the ground, his pulse pounding. The car below him was getting closer by the second.

Bear woke up in bed, his hair dripping with sweat and breathing like a racehorse. He sat up and looked around. It was mid-morning, and for some reason he didn't wake up with the sun. He got up and stumbled into the bathroom, noticing the red rims around his eyes. *I look like death warmed over.* He looked closer at his reflection in the mirror and saw bruises on his neck. He swallowed hard. Out of habit he switched on the TV to the local newscast and saw a car with its roof caved in, and the hair on the back of his neck stood up. The reporter was explaining what had happened. "Early this morning a local man apparently committed suicide by jumping out of a building downtown. I spoke to some of his co-workers, and none of them saw this coming. The victim's name is being withheld pending notifications of relatives."

After he turned off the spectacle, Bear just stared out the window for about a minute, staring at an eagle that had perched on a dead tree. *Maybe I'm still dreaming. This feels like the twilight zone. I can't seem to get a full breath of air. What does this thing want?*

Dagon stood in a large, dark room with a high ceiling. He counted nine platforms, each with a figure behind a desk. These were his judges, looking down on him from high above his position. There was a spotlight on Dagon, and he couldn't see the faces of the judges, but he was familiar with Baasha's voice…

Baasha: "Do you know why you're here, Dagon?"

Dagon began to answer but was cut off.

Baasha: "You've been warned about your heavy-handed techniques and your flair for the dramatic."

Dagon: "With all due respect, my techniques have worked well in the past."

Baasha: "We are not in the past!"

Dagon: "We no longer have the luxury of being subtle. The news of the portal has disrupted the timeline."

Baasha: "I believe you've lost your edge. You used a wrecking ball when you needed a scalpel. You pushed him too hard. He woke up, and now he's a threat."

Dagon: "There's still time to remedy the situation."

Baasha: "Convince me."

Dagon: "My specialty is finding weaknesses. I wrote the book. I have contingencies."

Baasha: "You better be right. You know how high the stakes are."

The Recipient

Zavan was pacing back and forth in his office as he was conferring with Kiandra. She could see that his concern for Bear's safety was weighing on him. "These attacks are getting dangerous. Dagon is evolving – he's growing more powerful. If I could just engage him directly…" Kiandra cut him off. "That's not an option right now." His eyes flashed with anger, "I'm sick and tired of games." She knew that Zavan took his missions seriously, but this one was personal, and she was concerned that his zeal could overrule his judgment. A sharp rebuke might send him over the edge. They were friends, but she was also his superior officer. "Zavan, you know there's a strategy in place that we can't always see. We don't know all the dynamics." Zavan raised his voice, "And McQuade could die while we're playing three dimensional chess! He needs our help!" He stormed out of the office. Kiandra felt it was better to just let him go. He said his piece – he just needed to blow off some steam. He's always been faithful – no need to doubt him now.

Bear was in a large formal dining room with a long wooden table, with none other than Dagon sitting at one end, cutting into a steak. As Bear was looking around, getting his bearings, Dagon spoke: "It's possible we got off on the wrong foot." Dagon motioned for Bear to sit down and eat – there was a plate prepared for him. "I know you can be reasonable." Bear ignored the food and looked directly at the mysterious figure in front of him and said in a tone that conveyed that he meant business, "I know what you are. It's over." Dagon put his fork down, and mockingly began clapping his hands, "Bravo, Mr. McQuade. It took you long enough. But it's far from over. I'm just getting warmed up." Bear continued, "I also know that your authority is limited. You're bluffing." Bear wasn't really sure how hard he wanted to push back. He also wasn't sure how powerful Dagon was, but he was tired of getting kicked around.

"Much of my work involves information... I know a great deal about you – your carefully guarded secrets, your hidden longings. I'm confident we can negotiate a win/win agreement." Bear said nothing; he just stared at Dagon, wondering where he was going with this. "Like I said earlier, I can help you. All these unfortunate occurrences that have been happening to you? I can make them all disappear. All you have to do is walk away. I hear you're good at that." Bear could see that this was just another move in this chess match. He was trying to get his way using any tactic he thought might work: threats, pressure points, intimidation, bribes... Bear took a step toward Dagon, and asked, "Why do you need me out of the way?" With a new level of confidence that surprised even himself, Bear lowered his voice to a whisper for effect. "You're going to lose." Bear's mannerisms reminded Dagon of Zavan, which infuriated him all the more – he exploded out of his chair, immediately morphing into full celestial mode as the room darkened and the smell of sulphur filled the air.. In an unearthly, guttural voice, he growled, "I will kill you!" By this time they were practically nose to nose. The evil radiating off him was almost overwhelming. Bear was worried that he might be consumed by it, but he did not back away. He didn't have to think hard, as the words came to him: "Maybe you will, but I've heard Shamayim

is beautiful this time of year." Dagon could see that his control techniques were not working, and was almost unable to contain his rage, "What is your answer?" Bear asked, "Final answer?" Dagon spat back, "Final answer." Bear looked at him right in the eyes and said, "Go to hell."

Bear snapped out of the trance with just enough time to realize that he was standing in the road near his mailbox, and a car was speeding toward him. He dove into the ditch, narrowly avoiding the car, which sped off down the road. Bear picked himself up, watched the car leave, and said, "Game on."

Dagon was in the same room where he had confronted Bear, and was seething. He spoke through clenched teeth: "If he wants a war, he's got one."

Dusty hadn't been ridden for a while, and Bear thought it might be a good way to get back control of his circumstances. Maybe it would be a break from all the weirdness – a way to ground him in reality. They started around dusk, heading west. He didn't mind riding after dark. He continued deeper into the forest. As a country boy, he knew there are different levels of quiet. There's ordinary quiet, there's forest quiet, and then there's forest quiet after dark. That kind of quiet allows, or forces you to think on a deeper level, and makes it easier to hear the voice of the Spirit. When he got to his favorite clearing, he dismounted and sat on a rock and soaked it in. It was rejuvenating.

For no apparent reason, Dusty got spooked and took off in the direction of home. Dusty never did that. It was really dark now, and Bear began walking in the direction of home.

Bear had no idea that about fifty yards away, Dagon was watching him. Next to him was a vicious-looking creature with four legs, shaggy fur, a muscular torso, dripping fangs, and a perpetual snarl. Dagon sensed that he was about to chalk up a win in his column, so he was unusually animated. He asked, "If you die in a dream, do you die in real life? Maybe there's a more appropriate question: Is it a dream or is it real? The answer is yes." He looked at the creature, snapped his fingers and said, "Go!" It took off down the path toward Bear, like a greyhound chasing a rabbit. Bear's eyes snapped wide open when he saw this creature coming at him at full speed and instinctively ran in the opposite direction. He looked over his shoulder and saw it closing in on him. 'God, help!' his mind screamed out, not realizing that he was indeed being watched over. In his office, watching on the big screen, Zavan was seeing it all, a look of desperation on his face. He wanted to help. He was created to help. Why was he being held back? Time was running out. Suddenly Kiandra burst through the office door holding a piece of paper in her hand. "We got the authorization – GO!" In a millisecond Zavan had morphed into full celestial mode and was heading to the forest like a beam of light. Just as Bear ran toward a stump and used it to launch himself upward toward a branch to try to avoid the beast, Zavan came in from the side and tackled it, sending them both sprawling over the forest floor. Bear let go of the branch after he saw that Zavan had given him a moment to escape. He didn't need to think twice - he hit the ground and kept running. Zavan and the beast squared off and sized each other up for a moment. The werewolf raised itself up to its full height – close to eight feet tall, then growled and lunged at Zavan, who deftly sidestepped the attack. The creature landed on all fours, then turned to chase Bear. It was incredibly quick. Zavan raced after it and grabbed it by the tail just as it was closing in, and whipped it around right into a tree.

Bear looked over his shoulder to see what was happening, and what he saw stopped him in his tracks. He blinked hard and shook his head, but the image in front of him didn't change: a ferocious, snarling, spitting werewolf facing off against an equally ferocious warrior angel. Bear met eyes briefly with Zavan, remembering where he had seen him before. That's all the time the creature needed to land a blow to the side of Zavan's head that sent him reeling. He got back up quickly as the werewolf covered at least twenty feet in one jump toward him. Zavan caught up in a flash and raised both fists up and came down on its head, dropping it to the ground, and wasted no time pummeling it with blow after blow. Although it was weakened, it had enough strength left to kick Zavan off and roll to its feet. Zavan picked up a fallen tree branch and swung it at the werewolf's back. A loud crack resonated through the forest, and the beast dropped to the ground. Zavan broke the branch over his knee and drove it through the monster's chest. It was over.

Bear somehow ended up in his truck next to the barn, where Dusty was sleeping. He was sweating and his pulse was elevated. He was in fight or flight mode, but he looked around and there was nothing to fight. He remembered the forest path he had been on, then Dusty running off. He remembered being attacked by... it all happened so fast. That was no animal he had ever seen before. And the angel - it felt too real to be a dream.

Zavan got up and looked down the path, where Dagon had been silently watching. He changed back to human form and walked toward Dagon, who was menacingly walking toward him. They stopped about ten feet apart. They could both see the other's matching forearm tattoo, reminding them of their history together.

Zavan: "Should have kept him on a leash."

Dagon: "They're expendable."

Zavan: "You've been busy."

Dagon just glared at him.

Zavan: "How did you find out about the portal?"

Dagon: "Secrets like that are difficult to keep."

There was an awkward pause.

Zavan: "Still working the plan?"

Dagon: "You call it a rebellion – I call it vision."

Zavan: "You can't win. You're just believing your own lies."

Dagon: "But think of the damage I can do."

Zavan: "Elohim has no weaknesses."

Dagon: "You're wrong, my old friend, he has two. He abides by his own rules, and he has compassion for these pathetic sacks of meat. It's such a great pleasure turning

*them against him. Now they blame him for their
suffering."*

Zavan was trying without success to understand this
mindset – this seething blind hatred that had consumed
his former friend. It served no purpose. It was hate for its
own sake.

Zavan: "To what end?"

*Dagon: "What part of revenge don't you understand?
Elohim's betrayal demands payback."*

*Zavan: "**His** betrayal?"*

*Dagon: He had our eternal adoration, but he wanted
more. He created them in his own image, then fell in love
with them. We were replaced by animated mud."*

Zavan: "You're out of your mind."

*Dagon: "And what are you? Always obeying orders
without question; the noble hero…. You may be content
taking a back seat to our inferiors, but I'm not. I'm going
to let you in on a little secret: humans are not worth your
effort. They will ultimately disappoint you."*

Zavan: "You were my greatest disappointment."

*Dagon: "You know as well as I that things can never be
as they were. In his great 'wisdom', the creator has only
offered redemption to humans."*

Zavan: "Would you take it if it were offered?"

They stared at each other. Zavan thought he saw
remorse in Dagon's eyes for a brief moment, then
Dagon slowly dissolved into the darkness. Zavan sensed
a presence behind him, so he turned around to find
Kiandra walking toward him. Before he could ask why
she was there, she said, "You've been summoned."
There was no hint in her voice or demeanor of whether
it was good or bad.

The Recipient

They dissolved in a flash of light and appeared in a place very familiar to Zavan – a court made of crystal. It was breathtaking, but in a different way – there was a seriousness about this place. This is where decisions were made. They began walking to the imposing double doors. As they crossed the threshold into the huge foyer, Zavan said, a little defensively, "I just did what I had to do."

They entered a chamber with four shimmering beings seated behind desks. Zavan addressed the beings, "I'm prepared to defend my actions. My charge is still in danger. He needs help." Even thought Zavan had received authorization to intervene on Bear's behalf, part of him wondered if he had taken it too far. Is that why he was here? Were they going to reprimand him for getting too personally involved? The spokesman for the group responded, "Zavan, you have shown great courage and dedication. You persevered even you didn't understand." Zavan was taken aback by the compliment. He glanced at Kiandra, who showed no indication that she knew what this was about, then back to the group. The spokesman continued, "You were chosen for this mission because of your passion. If you believe your charge needs more protection... and if you think he's ready..." he nodded his head toward the back wall, which opened up, revealing a small, ornate box with a brilliant light shining from it. Zavan said nothing, but walked over to the box, then glanced back at the spokesman, who nodded his head. Zavan reached into the box and pulled out three huge gemstones. The stones of fire!

The Recipient

Zavan wasted no time in carrying out his mission. He showed up in the middle of the night while Bear was sound asleep. "Bear!", he said, "Wake up." Bear was immediately awake, and before he could even ask any questions, Zavan said, "Get up. Follow me." Zavan touched his arm, and they disappeared in a flash of light, reappearing in a bright room that reminded him of the dream he had earlier. "Must be dreaming." He said. "This is not a dream." Zavan replied. "There's something you're going to need." He opened his hand, revealing the brilliantly shining gemstones. Bear could feel the energy coming from them. From what he remembered, they carried the very presence of God. Zavan said, "The stones of fire." Bear also knew that Lucifer had some connection with the stones. He said, "Didn't Lucifer…" he searched for the right words, but Zavan interjected, "He misused them." Bear instinctively knew that there was danger involved. "What if I misuse them?" Zavan probed, "Do you trust yourself?" Bear thought for a moment, let out a sigh of disappointment, and said, "No." His eyes fell to the ground. He wasn't worthy of this. Zavan said, "Good answer." Bear looked up at him, surprised. "Zavan continued, "Only a fool trusts himself. You know who to trust. You're ready." Zavan put the stones against Bear's chest and waited for his okay. He knew there was no going back after this. He took a deep breath and said, "Do it." Without hesitating, Zavan pushed the stones into Bear's chest. Bear inhaled sharply and his head was forcefully thrown back. He felt electricity going through his body. It wasn't exactly painful, but very intense. He felt the energy growing stronger and stronger, until everything went black.

The Recipient

Chapter fourteen

Kidnapped

Jennifer didn't spend much time at the county library,
she preferred upscale boutiques and coffee shops.
Almost everything she needed was online, but the library
offered something she couldn't get at home – secrecy.
Given her suspicions about Reece, and the strange things
going on, she felt the need to dig into his background.
Who knows whether he was keeping tabs on her
internet sites, phone conversations... maybe she was just
being paranoid, but nobody could track her at the
library.

She went through the rows of bookcases to an obscure
door. The sign above it read 'archives'. She went through
it, down the stairs, and looked around. It felt like she was
back in the sixties – or earlier: racks of newspapers,
magazines, microfiche machines... where to start.
As she was searching old newspaper articles for anything
related to Reece, she noticed a very old article in a
frame, hanging on the wall. The headline caught her
attention, so she quickly made a copy of the article and
went back to her research.

Bear was trying to focus on the job at hand – completing
the work on the Bernell's lower level. It was not easy to
stay focused, considering all that had happened in the
past few days. He still wondered if he would wake up
and find that it was all a dream. Jennifer approached
him, looking worried and carrying a laptop. Bear asked,

"What is it?" She replied, "I did some digging." She turned the laptop around, showing Bear an archived web page of an old news story about a local businessman's wife who died mysteriously in a boating accident. The picture attached to the story was – Reece Bernell. Bear looked at her and said, "And you think…" She cut in, "I don't think, Bear, I know. It's like my intuition is working again. It's not safe for us here, but it's not safe for us to leave, either. He'll find us. He's like a pit bull; when he latches on, he doesn't let go. If I try to leave, I know he'll kill me." Before she could continue, Missy entered the room, looking scared. They turned their attention to her, and Jennifer asked, "Missy, what's wrong?"

Over the next few minutes, Missy related exactly what had happened in the warehouse, the night terrors, the fear of a little girl not knowing what to do or who to talk to… Jennifer grabbed Missy and hugged her so tight she could barely breathe. Bear's mind was reeling. *I have to do something. I was brought here for a reason. But what? What does Reece know?* Bear turned to Jennifer, "Are there cameras in the warehouse?" She replied, "Yes, it has cameras, but I don't know where they're located. Reece goes through the security footage at the end of the week, depending on how busy he is. Sometimes he copies it to a jump drive and does it at home." Bear continued, "I wish we knew if she had been caught on camera." After thinking about it for a moment, Jennifer said, "I have to go there and see what I can find out." She had Missy draw map of the warehouse, and where she was standing. Missy put a circle where she was when it happened. Jennifer looked at Bear resolutely and said, "I'll be back as soon as I can."

Bear said, "I don't like this." Jennifer responded with, "I'm the only one who can do this... Bear, if this goes sideways..." He interrupted, "Don't even think that way."

At the warehouse, Reece was busy at his desk, but not too busy to notice his wife pulling into the parking lot. Jennifer walked into the foyer, saw the area Missy pointed out, and got hit with a sick feeling. The camera was pointed right at that spot. Now it was only a matter of time until Reece knew – unless he already did and was playing it cool. She would have to find out. Reece came out of his office, "What's a nice girl like you doing in a place like this?" There was that old Reece Bernell charm. Jennifer faked her best smile and said, "Hi honey, I thought I'd bring you some lunch." She had stopped at a fast food place on the way just in case, and she handed him the bag and kissed him. As they walked into his office, Jennifer casually asked, "So are you staying busy?" Reece answered, "Oh, you know... there's always something to do. Well, maybe you don't know – you've never shown a lot of interest in my work. Anyway, it's almost the weekend, so I'll have to watch the security footage tonight," nodding at his keychain with the jump drive on it. "Now I just have to look over some paperwork Gunner turned in." Jennifer saw an opportunity, "Why don't you come home early? You're always working so hard." She was able to convince Reece to come home for a while, without coming on too strong. She was already pushing her luck. They drove separately, so Jennifer called Bear and told him the plan, "... if I can get you the keychain, you'll have to erase that part of the footage." Bear understood, "Okay, but I'll need some time." Jennifer responded, "I'll have it on the table outside the master bedroom. Get it back there in twenty minutes."

In the master bedroom, Jennifer, dressed in her red silky nightgown, had her arms around Reece's neck. She pulled away and said, "I just remembered something. I'll be right back." She went into the dressing area and swiped his key ring, then quietly opened the hall door and carefully put the key ring onto the table. She saw Bear peering out from behind a pillar and nodded to him before going back and spraying herself with a generous amount of 'Pleasures' – her favorite fragrance. Bear moved silently toward the table after the door was shut. He lifted it gingerly, trying to be as quiet as possible. He got back downstairs and inserted the jump drive into his laptop. He didn't know what he would do if it was password protected. Amazingly, it wasn't. He was able to bring up the footage. There were a lot of files under the heading of 'securitycam'. He didn't know if he would be able to go through all of them in time, but he found the one he needed. He saw the shot of Missy hiding and deleted the file. He glanced at the clock, and his time was almost up, so he pulled out the jump drive and snuck back upstairs as quickly as he could without making noise and put the key ring back on the table. The next part was up to Jennifer, who opened the door just seconds later and grabbed them. Back in the bedroom, Reece was looking at his phone, which gave her the chance to get the key ring back where she found it.

Not too long after that, Reece was headed out the front door with a concerned look on his face. Jennifer said, "Where are you going, honey?" She wanted him gone, but it looked like he knew something. He said, "I'm going back to the office; there's something I need to check on." She asked him, "Can't it wait until next week?" He replied, "I didn't make a fortune by letting things slide until next week."

As Reece drove away, Bear came up the stairs. Jennifer said, "I think he noticed something was missing. When he gets back to his computer, he'll find out." Bear took a deep breath and said, "I was hoping this would buy us more time. Why don't you get your stuff packed, and I'll meet you out front in five minutes." They both understood there would be no turning back after this. They drove separately to the nearest strip mall and dropped off Jennifer's car, then the three of them got into Bear's pickup and drove off.

Reece didn't waste any time getting to the warehouse and made a beeline for his computer. He had noticed that some files were missing right around the time of 'the incident'. That couldn't be a coincidence. He had learned to be suspicious. He opened up the program and started watching the security footage. He sat back in his chair when he saw the little trespasser on camera. Unknown to Reece, Dagon was looking over his shoulder and said, "Looks like it's time for another boating accident." Reece turned away from the monitor and said, "Looks like it's time for another boating accident... and I was just getting used to them." After sending a text message to an associate, he headed out the door.

Bear, Jennifer and Missy arrived at Bear's house and went inside. Bear said, "You should be safe here for a while. Just in case, though…" Bear opened the bookcase and showed them the secret room, and how they could monitor the security feed with the tablet in the room. Missy, who was usually upbeat, had a worried look in her eyes. Bear didn't want to leave her like that, but he had to go. "There's something I need to get. I'll be back as soon as possible." Bear drove off to the outdoor sports store a few miles away. In the hunting section he found what he was looking for: a box of buckshot for his twelve-gage shotgun.

Minutes after Bear left, Reece pulled into the driveway. He didn't like the feeling that he had been played, and wasted no time getting Bear's home address. Jennifer saw him and got herself and Missy into the panic room and shut the door. Reece walked up to the front door and looked around. Jennifer realized she had forgotten to lock the front door after Bear left. Not that a locked door would stop Reece. He opened it and walked inside, gun drawn, as Jennifer and Missy were watching him on the security feed. Jennifer turned to Missy and put her finger to her lips. Reece remembered his first conversation with Bear, that he had mentioned something about panic rooms. Panic rooms. He walked around the living room, examining the walls, then he pulled out his phone and made a call. Jennifer gasped almost loud enough for Reece to hear through the wall, as she dove into her purse to find her phone and shut it off, but it was too late. It rang loud enough for Reece to hear, which led him to the hidden door. As it opened, Jennifer and Missy stared at him in terror. He ordered them out of the house and put them in his car, but before getting in, he walked over to the corral. Missy screamed as they heard a gunshot. Reece calmly got into the car a few seconds later and took off down the road.

Bear drove into his driveway with an uneasy feeling in the pit of his stomach. When he got out of his truck, he saw Dusty on the ground, with blood coming out of his head. The realization of what was happening hit him like a freight train. He spun around and ran to the house, where he saw the door open to the panic room. His breathing started to speed up and he felt dizzy and said, "I should have been here." He walked out the front door and sat down on the steps, recalling the motorcycle incident from years ago. "What was I thinking? Everything I touch turns to crap." Zavan, who was watching this play out, could feel the panic and hopelessness setting in. He knew he had to help Bear keep it together, or the whole plan would come crashing down. Looking at Bear, he said, "Don't go there!" Bear felt his entire life falling apart. *De ja vu*. He whispered, "It's happening again." Zavan raised his voice, "I'm serious, Bear, you can't do this to yourself!" Bear walked toward the barn and collapsed in the middle of the driveway, "Why would I even think I could…" His breathing escalated and he had a look of panic in his eyes. Zavan, almost in a panic himself, yelled, "BEAR! Snap out of it!" Bear lifted his head and looked around, as if he had heard something, then shook his head and said quietly, "I got nothing left." He was almost catatonic. Zavan had to do something. Bear continued, "If they're not dead already, I'd probably just get them killed." Zavan shot upward like a beam of light. Bear stumbled out to the barn, in the back, where his old junked out convertible sat. It was almost like his mind had been hijacked. He spoke to the car, "You just sit there…" He picked up a sledgehammer that was close by and raised it over his head to smash the car's hood. He raised his voice, "You worthless piece of…" He stopped in mid-swing, because he thought he heard something. He dropped the sledgehammer, and fell to his knees. In the silence, he heard it again – the voice of a little boy. "Daddy?" His eyes snapped open, and he remembered seeing his son – it was like remembering a dream, but he knew it was real. Nobody could tell him otherwise. It was as if a bolt of lightning hit him and fried whatever was controlling him. He said, "It's not about me." Missy came to his mind. He remembered her playing the violin just a day ago. He couldn't give up. No excuses this time. He ran to his truck and got in. "How do I find them?" He thought out loud. He looked in the back seat, and there was Bernell's file. He grabbed it and looked inside and saw a copy of the building permit. He thought for a second and started up the truck and sped away.

He arrived at the county courthouse, double-parked and ran in. He found the permits division and walked through the door into a room filled with file cabinets and computers, and a frumpy-looking woman behind the counter wearing bifocals. Bear put on a smile and approached her, "Hi – I just pulled a permit for my client, and I didn't get all the information I needed;

would you mind pulling that file for me again?" He handed her the building permit. She handed Bear an official-looking file that he took to a table and sat down. After scanning it he said quietly, "Bingo - lake house," and wrote down the address.

In the den at the lake house, Jennifer was duct-taped to a chair, and Missy was quietly sitting in a chair next to her, both looking at Reece. Jennifer couldn't hold it back, "You don't have to do this. At least let her go." Reece responded without looking up from his paperwork, "Actually I do. My rule is no loose ends. Oh, and this might not make you feel better, but it's not your fault. Unfortunately, your daughter saw something she shouldn't have." Reece looked at his watch and walked out the door and down to the dock. As he boarded the boat, he said to one of his men, "Where are the gas cans?" The man quickly replied, "Gunner went to find them." Reece sighed and said under his breath, "Gunner couldn't find his own ass with both hands and a flashlight." The man asked Reece, "Are we still leaving at sundown?" Reece responded, "Nothing's changed. And we were never here."

Bear drove to the lake house and circled around to the vacant land next to the property. He parked his truck behind a treed area that provided cover. He got out and grabbed his shotgun and field glasses from the back seat. Before he shut the door, he breathed out a request: "I need your help to save them. Give me your strategy. Send someone to help me." Bear didn't really expect God to send someone to help him. His faith wasn't that strong, but he figured it couldn't hurt to ask. Isn't that what you do before you go into battle? He made his way to a vantage point where he had an unobstructed view of the house. As he was looking through the binoculars, he heard the unmistakable sound of a bullet being chambered in a semiautomatic pistol, and then a hushed voice coming from behind him, "Drop the gun." Bear froze, then slowly put the gun on the ground and put his hands on his head and turned around. Bear recognized him as Rob, one of Reece's men. Rob asked in a lowered voice, "Why have you been meeting with Jennifer?" Bear answered quietly, "We're… having an affair." " Rob looked amused and said, "You're a terrible liar." Bear was out of ideas. "You here to rescue her?" Rob questioned. Bear didn't see the point of denying the obvious, "That was the plan." Rob responded, "What do you know about Bernell's operation?" Bear almost laughed, but kept his voice low, "Operation?! Nothing! I'm just the handyman. And why are we whispering?" Rob thought for a second, and said, "Get down." They both got on the ground, out of the line of sight. Something was not adding up. This guy was not who he appeared to be. Bear asked, "Why are *you* hiding?" Rob sighed again, and said, "I'm undercover." Bear gave him a quizzical look. "Mossad," Rob told him. Bear was even more confused, "Mossad? As in Israeli special forces Mossad?" Rob confirmed, "That's the one." Bear asked, "What's Mossad's interest in this?" Before Rob could respond, a light went on in Bear's head. "Of course – black market Israeli artifacts." Bear focused back on the house, "I think he's going to kill them." Rob filled in the blanks – "That's why I'm here. I bugged his office, and I found out the girl witnessed a murder. I would have called the police, but by the time I answered all their questions it would be too late." He continued, "We need a diversion." He scanned the property for a few seconds and said, "You see that shed? I need you to set it on fire, then get out of there. I'll get the girls and meet you back here. I'll probably need you to lay down some ground cover." Rob remembered he wasn't talking to a soldier, and looked at Bear, who replied, "Got it – that means shoot at the bad guys." Rob got a worried look on his face and asked, "You ever been in a firefight?" As Bear picked up his shotgun, he said, "Just point and click, right?" Under his breath, Rob added, "And pray."

Bear had gotten into the shed and splashed gas all over. He looked through the window before he started the fire. Seeing nobody outside, he lit the gas and ran into the woods. Soon the shed was engulfed in flames. Gunner was the first to notice it and ran to the house, "Boss, the shed's on fire!" They both ran out to the shed, where Reece's other hired gun was spraying the fire with a fire extinguisher without much success. Reece turned to Gunner and yelled, "In the boathouse! There are fire extinguishers in the boathouse!" Gunner ran to the boathouse and brought back two extinguishers. Reece said, "The last thing we need is to call attention to ourselves."

While they were occupied, Rob crept into the house and found Jennifer and Missy. He said to them, "We're getting you out of here." Jennifer was surprised and confused and asked, "We?" Rob answered, "Your handyman friend. Now let's go." While they were heading to the front door, Bear was doing some last-second recalculations in his head: speed, distance, number and location of bad guys… It was time to improvise. He drove his pickup across the yard, mowing down hedges as he went. He stopped and pointed his shotgun at the corner of the house, while Rob, Missy and Jennifer ran toward the truck. Reece and Gunner ran toward the action, but a shotgun blast kept them hidden around the corner. As they ran to the truck, Gunner took a wild shot around the corner that hit Rob, who found cover and returned fire, and yelled "Go!" at the top of his voice. Bear gunned it, while Reece ran to his car. Rob saw his opportunity – a propane tank near the corner of the house; he took his shot, and the resulting explosion sent a fireball fifty feet into the air.

Bear didn't have much of a head start, and Reece was gaining on him. He yelled at Missy and Jennifer, "Get down!" Bear knew he couldn't outrun a performance sedan on pavement, so he turned down a gravel road at breakneck speed. After going over several curves and hills, he couldn't shake Reece. Bear looked at Jennifer and said, "Take the wheel." She slid over, while he grabbed his shotgun and managed to point it backwards out the window. Reece saw the gun and backed off, but a big bump in the road jarred the gun out of Bear's hands. Time for plan B. He got out on the runner boards and jumped into the back of the pickup. He maneuvered himself under a hay bale, and kicked it over the back, causing Reece to lose control and plow into the ditch. That gave them time to put some distance between them.

After fighting his way through the air bags that had deployed, Reece immediately got on his phone. "I want everything you got on this guy: family, finances, what websites he visits, where he gets his haircut – everything." The voice on the other side of the call said, "I'll have it to you as soon as I can." Reece replied, "I need it before then." Under normal circumstances Reece was not a patient man, but after this humiliating setback by some loser nobody, he was seething.

The Recipient

The Recipient

Chapter fifteen

Dead End

July 1901

Olive was in the middle of a lake, all alone in a rowboat, when the sky quickly filled with dark storm clouds. The wind picked up, and the waves started crashing into the small boat. She glanced around – she was a long way from shore. This didn't feel right. She had to get to shore NOW! She began rowing, pulling at the oars with all her strength. The wind was fighting her, so she decided to try to go diagonally. The waves were getting higher, threatening to swamp the boat, and she felt panic creeping in. A lightning bolt struck, illuminating the entire lake for a moment. She counted, one thousand one, one thousand two, one thou- then she heard the thunder, so loud it almost knocked her off the seat. The lightning was just a half mile away. She continued to struggle toward the shore. Then she saw it – something big surfaced near the boat. She looked on the other side of the boat, and saw the face of a man looking right into her eyes. He was completely submerged, and he had fins where his legs should have been. Olive felt a stab of fear grip her like she had never known. She felt most of her strength drain out of her, through her eyes. This sinister creature reached for her hand. She wasn't able to snatch it away in time, and it got ahold of her and started pulling her into the water. She tried to resist, but she felt like she had nothing left. Her face was getting closer to the water, when she heard that familiar sound – the violin. The next thing she knew, she was in her bed, heart pounding, drenched in sweat. Strange - she could still hear the music. She followed the sound to Shannon's bedroom – she was playing violin by candlelight. She stopped when she saw her mother; "Mom, are you okay?" Olive didn't say anything – she just went over and hugged her little girl. After Olive had recovered, she got her journal out and sketched out what she remembered. That face, and those sinister eyes... something she would never forget.

Kiandra burst into Zavan's office and said, "We need to talk. The situation is escalating." Zavan said, "More like exploding." Kiandra continued, "You need to stay close to McQuade; he needs your help now more than ever." Zavan didn't need any encouragement to step up. He lived for this. Kiandra thought briefly about what she was going to say next. The timing had to be right. "*And this moves up the timetable.*" Zavan looked up, his interest peaked, "You mean...?" Kiandra smiled, "It's a go for tonight!" It had been a long time since he had done a direct intervention, but he was more than ready. "Full celestial mode, I assume." He said, knowing full well what the answer would be. Kiandra nodded. "It's always a risk, but they're forcing our hand."

The Recipient

Bear, Jennifer and Missy were in the truck, driving down a gravel road. Bear handed his phone to Jennifer and said, "Take the batteries out of our phones. We have to go low tech now. I don't know if they can track us, but I'd rather be safe than sorry."

Jennifer: "How did you locate us?"

Bear: "I followed a hunch. Reece said something about a lake house, so I looked up the property records at city hall."

Jennifer: "What about the guy who rescued us? I thought he worked for Reece."

Bear: "He told me he was undercover. I didn't have much choice but to believe him."

Jennifer: "I hope he made it."

Bear: "I have a feeling his training kicked in."

Reece walked into his office and put his hands to his mouth and took a deep breath. As Dagon was pacing, he said, "A hundred large buys a lot of loyalty." Reece said out loud, "I'll put out a reward through my network," as if he came up with the idea himself. He got on his phone and made the calls.

Bear pulled his truck into a strip mall on the outskirts of the city. They all went into a convenience store. In the pawn shop next door, a big seedy-looking man looked at an email on his phone and said, "Whoa! A hundred thousand dollars!" He glanced out at the parking lot and saw something that captured his interest. As Bear was walking back to the truck, he was met by the pawn shop employee. He was standing right in Bear's path. He looked at the picture on his cell phone, then at Bear, and said, "I smell money. You're coming with me." He pulled back his jacket to reveal a pistol tucked in his pants. Jennifer walked out of the convenience store and saw what was happening and she grabbed Missy and pulled her back into the store. Bear noticed a crude tattoo on the man's forearm as he showed Bear the picture on his phone. "Don't tell me this isn't you." Bear had to think quickly. His heart was racing, but he managed to keep his voice steady, "So… Chuck (his name was printed on his shirt), I have a question for you. Do you have a permit for that .38 special?" Chuck didn't answer; he just cleared his throat. Glancing across the parking lot, Bear continued, "You see that café over there? I'm going to meet a friend there in four minutes. His name is Sargent Miller." Bear paused to let that sink in. Chuck didn't reveal anything, but said, "I'm getting good money for you." Bear shot back, "It's going to be hard to spend it on cell block D. I don't think you want to go back inside, because this makes you an accessory. And they will catch you… Chuck." At this point there was a bead of sweat running down Chuck's left temple, and his eyes were darting around. Bear continued, "Three minutes. Now I'm going to get in my truck and go meet my friend, and when I turn around, I don't want to see you." Bear got in the truck and when he looked back, Chuck was gone. He picked up Missy and Jennifer and drove off.

Bear: "We have to go to the police. They can protect you."

Jennifer: "I don't think so. His tentacles may reach into the police department."
Bear: "I don't know that we have a choice."
Jennifer: "But we have to be careful about who we trust."
Bear: "There's a pay phone. I didn't know they were still around."   Bear pulled over and opened his door.
Jennifer: "You never did listen to me."
Bear: "Maybe you should have asked James Bond to help you. But you didn't; you asked me. And this is me helping you."

He got out and made the call. Jennifer heard the tail end of his phone conversation: "Okay, I'll be at the corner of Snelling and Aimes in half an hour. I'll be wearing a black jacket."

They arrived at the location a little early and parked about a block away. Jennifer pointed to the corner and said, "Didn't you say you'd be wearing a black jacket?" Bear looked and saw a man wearing a black jacket. Wrong place, wrong time. They heard a loud crack, then the man collapsed. Jennifer inhaled sharply and covered her mouth with her hands. Bear forced himself out of his shock, put his truck in gear and got out of there. They were both beginning to realize they were in over their heads. They had been set up. Jennifer was almost hysterical, saying, "They killed him... they killed him." Bear said, "Either that detective was on Reece's payroll or his phone was bugged." Jennifer added, "And that man paid for it." Bear felt like the guilt of that man's death would crush him. All he could do was keep going and try to not let the same thing happen to Missy and Jennifer.

Reece was nothing if not strategic. He knew how to play the public relations game. He could make the authorities work for him. He drove to the police station and started his 'traumatized husband and father routine'. He told them about this psycho who had weaseled his way into their house and kidnapped his wife and daughter. He's a very dangerous man… They bought it hook, line and sinker, and put out an amber alert.

Soon Bear pulled into a gas station. As he was looking for something to eat, he noticed that the clerk was glued to the TV screen behind the counter. It was an amber alert with Bear's picture on the screen. 'Be on the lookout for this man; he has allegedly kidnapped a woman and her daughter. He was last seen driving a dark four door pickup.' Bear tried to walk casually toward the exit, while he kept an eye on the cashier, who was trying to look like he wasn't paying attention. He picked up his phone as soon as Bear got out the door. Bear got in the truck and said, "Get down," and sped away from the gas station. "What is it?" Jennifer asked. Bear responded with a frown, "I just kidnapped you – amber alert."
Jennifer: "This just gets better and better."
Bear: "Look, I'm making this up as I go. If you have any ideas, now would be a great time to put them on the table."

A few minutes went by as they were driving, trying not to attract any attention. Before long they were on a country road with no one in sight.

Jennifer couldn't keep it in any longer. "As long as I've known you, bad things seem to follow you around. Why did I think you were sent to help me?" Bear slammed on the brakes and pulled to the side of the road and said, "What did you say?" Jennifer got out of the truck and slammed the door and walked into the ditch. Bear got out and followed her. She couldn't handle it in any more. All her pent-up emotion had to come out, and it wasn't pretty. Jennifer yelled at Bear, "Look, I just found out my husband is a gangster who is now trying to kill me and my daughter. We just got some poor guy killed, and now the police are after us."

Bear: "I'm aware of that."

Jennifer: "You know what? You were right. If I want to ruin my life I call you!"

Bear took a breath to respond but she wasn't done.

Jennifer: "If you hadn't shown up, I bet none of this would have happened."

Bear: "You want to leave?"

Jennifer defiantly answered, "Yeah, I do."

Bear spun around and went back to the truck and grabbed her backpack, threw it to her and said, "Bon voyage." Jennifer glanced over at the truck where Missy was sitting, watching them. She knew Bear had called her bluff.

Bear: "Where are you going to go? How will you protect Missy? I'll tell you what – You want to go, then go, but Missy stays with me."

Jennifer: "You're going to kidnap my daughter for real?"

Bear: "You tell me, who will she be safer with? It's not always about you, Jenn."

Jennifer: "Don't call me Jenn."

Bear: "You know what? We're going to do something a little crazy. We're going to ask Missy what she thinks." Jennifer exclaimed, "What?" Bear continued, "Why not? I'm a lost cause and you're out of control; maybe she's the one person here who can think clearly." Jennifer folded her arms and spat out, "Fine." They went over to the truck and opened the door. Jennifer gave Bear a dirty look and began, "Sweetheart, we want to know – *I* want to know what you think. Should we split up or stick together?" Missy looked at Bear, then back to her mom, and said, "He's part of the plan, mom." Without another word, they were back in the truck, driving down the road, both feeling a little chastised. "Hmm." Bear said, as if he had just been hit in the back of his head with an idea. "I think I know where we can go."

The pickup pulled into Neal's driveway and stopped. They got out and walked up to the front door and knocked. Neal opened it almost immediately and exchanged a knowing look with Bear. They went inside and made introductions. While Missy was watching her favorite nature show in Neal's living room, the two filled in Neal with their escapades. Bear said, "...so we're in deep sludge. This guy is bad, and he's well connected." Neal put his head in his hands and thought for a moment. He cocked his head and asked, "How far are you willing to take this?" Jennifer asked, "What do you

have in mind?" Neal calmly shot back in his southern drawl, "Desperate times – desperate measures."
Bear: "Are you talking about a pre-emptive strike?
Neal: "Are you willing to do it?"
Bear: "There's got to be another way."
Jennifer: "We're not killers. We have to live with the consequences of what we're about to do."
Neal: "The operative word being live." He paused for a moment. "I did see something once… it's a long shot."
Jennifer: "At this point I don't think there are any bad ideas."
Neal: "I'm going to have to kill you."
Jennifer's eyebrows shot up, and she looked at Bear.
Bear: "I think I know where he's going with this."
Looking back at Neal, he said, "We fake her death."
Neal: "It would have to be very convincing. Investigators these days can spot a staged crime scene a mile away."
Jennifer: "Sort of a witness relocation program."
Neal: "Self-imposed. I have some experience in that area."
With that revelation, Bear suddenly understood Neal's reticence to talk about his past, but now was not the time to talk about that.
Bear: "What about new ID's?"
Neal: "I know a guy."
Jennifer turned to Bear: "What about you? Even if he thinks I'm dead, he'll still come after you."
Bear: "That did cross my mind. I guess I don't really have a choice. Today is as good a day as any to die."
Without a word, Neal left the room and came back with tubes and intravenous bags.
Neal: "Let's get started."

The Recipient

Bear: "Where did you get those?"
Neal: "You don't want to know."
Before long, the three of them were intermittently
clenching their right hands to coax out the blood faster.
Incredibly, it didn't bother Missy. With all she had been
through, maybe her threshold for drama was growing.
Jennifer: "You guys are from two different worlds; how
did you meet?"
Neal: "If we make it through this – sorry, when we
make it through this, I'll tell you the whole story."

They arrived at the abandoned building Neal had
chosen and went in. After they found a good spot, they
started splattering the blood around, making it look like
a crime scene. The plan was for Neal to call in an
anonymous tip to the police about a murder that had
taken place. The police would confirm that Jennifer,
Missy and Bear were the victims with a DNA test. Neal
had mixed the blood with plasma to create more
volume. No one could survive losing that much blood.
The normal DNA tests wouldn't show that extra plasma
had been added. Bear wasn't used to this kind of
subterfuge. It seemed awfully dark. Was this the right
thing to do? A little late to be asking. There didn't seem
to be any other way out. They had talked about going to
the feds, but Neal put the kibosh on that idea. Federal
agents are no more immune to bribes than local law
enforcement.

When they were finished and heading back to the cars,
Neal said, "I'll call in an anonymous tip in a few days."

Bear said, "It's too dangerous for us all to be together. And it's better if you don't know where we are. I'll call you tomorrow." Neal asked, "Is there anything else I can do to help?" Bear looked at the Hummer and said, "I think there is."

The Recipient

Chapter sixteen

Secret of the Portal

Jennifer, Bear and Missy were driving in Neal's Hummer over a divided bridge, when an alert officer in a police car going the opposite direction noticed Bear and flipped the siren on. He had to go to the end of the bridge to turn around, which gave Bear time to hustle over the next hill and turn off on a side road. They drove for a few minutes before hearing a helicopter. Looking backwards, Jennifer could see it was following them. They knew better than to try to outrun a helicopter. Bear pulled into a heavily wooded area, "I know these woods – we'll have a better chance on foot." He parked the conspicuous vehicle under a tree, and they got out and started down a trail. Minutes later the helicopter landed nearby, and three deputies got out and ran over to the Hummer. The leader put his hand on the hood and said, "They don't have much of a head start. Let's get going."

Jennifer, Bear and Missy got winded from running, so they stopped for a rest by a hillside, where Missy found an opening to a shallow cave. They were running out of options, so they went into it to hide. There wasn't much room in the cave, and it felt like the walls were closing in so Bear again made a request, "Please… send help." A spider began to shoot back and forth over the cave opening. Under his breath, Bear said, "I asked for help, and you send a spider?" While it continued to weave its web, Missy picked up on what was happening. She said in an excited whisper, "It's closing us in!" Less than a minute later, they heard the deputies approaching. One of them noticed the opening and said, "Should we check out this cave? Someone could hide in there." The leader responded, "See that spider web? Nothing's been in there for days. Let's keep moving and meet up with the others." The other deputy asked, "Should I go back and cover the vehicle?" The leader replied, "No, we need you with us. There's no way they would double back. I'd bet my badge on it."

After the deputies were gone, the three cautiously came out of the cave and started back to the Hummer. After they had walked about three minutes, Bear saw something on the path directly in front of them that made him jump. It was a huge, snarling black dog with glowing red eyes, like a Doberman on steroids. It disappeared as quickly as it appeared. Jennifer asked, "What's wrong?" Bear looked at her incredulously and asked, "Didn't you see it?" She didn't know what he was talking about. She replied, "See what?" "Never mind," Bear said, just shaking it off.

 None of them knew that Dagon was immersed in a powerful conjuring spell at that moment. There were candles on his heavy oak table forming a circle, with a silver cup in the center with some foul liquid in it. He was reciting an ancient language. He was reaping the benefit of centuries of work, tapping into ancient networks he had built, weaving the spiritual and physical realms together for his own purposes.

As they continued on the path, Bear felt all his senses heighten. He hoped he wouldn't see it again. How do you fight a hell hound? He would find out all too quickly. It appeared again in front of them. Jennifer could see Bear react, but couldn't see why. "What do you see?" Bear stood stock still and whispered back, "It's right there!" Missy sniffed and said, "What's that smell?" As the creature inched closer, Bear said, "Sulfur. Get back!" It crouched low and emitted a guttural growl that made the hair on Bear's neck stand on end. Suddenly it turned and lunged at Missy. Bear caught the devil dog in the rib cage with a kick, knocking it off balance onto the grass. Instantly it was back up, snarling at Bear.

Zavan was once again watching on the monitor in his office, holding his breath. "Come on, Bear. This one's yours."

As the dog leaped at Bear, he sacrificed his left forearm to its gaping jaws, so he could force it down onto the ground, and use his right arm to hold it down while he got behind it. That might have worked on an ordinary dog, but this one was too strong – it pushed Bear over and landed on top of him. It went berserk and lunged at his throat. Bear was using all his strength to hold it back, but he knew he couldn't last much longer.

Zavan felt like he was in the fight of his life. "Use your authority!" He yelled at the screen.

Suddenly Bear felt as if time had slowed down. The snarling creature was still coming closer to his throat, but an unearthly calm came over him, and he looked into the eyes of the hound and issued a command: "Go back to where you came from." It instantly closed its mouth and stopped snarling, then backed away and bolted into the underbrush. The momentary sense of authority and serenity he felt was gone. Now he was feeling the aftermath of a life or death encounter with a supernatural killing machine. Jennifer and Missy rushed over to Bear and helped him up. They saw that his left arm was bleeding, and Jennifer asked, "What happened?" Bear was breathing like a locomotive and had a wild, almost panicked look in his eyes. He opened his mouth to talk, but nothing would come out. He just shook his head. Finally he managed to speak: "That was no dream."

A short time later they were back in the Hummer and they had pulled into an old farmstead. Bear said, "I know this place; nobody's lived here for a long time." He drove up to the barn and told Jennifer, "I'll open the door, you drive it in." No sooner did he open the door than they heard a helicopter approaching. He motioned for her to hurry. As he shut the door, the chopper flew overhead, and Bear heaved a sigh of relief. As they looked around, Missy said, "I'm hungry." Bear said, "I bet there's some food in here." He found a bag of trail mix and gave it to Missy and sat down by her. As she was eating, Bear asked her, "Hey Missy, how come you're so good at playing the violin?"
Missy: "I heard my teacher tell my mom that I'm a prodigy. I wasn't supposed to hear it though"
Bear: "Why not?"

Missy: "I don't know. I don't know what a prodigy is. Maybe they think I won't practice as much."
Bear: "I'm guessing you like to practice."
Missy: "Sometimes I feel my heart tingle when I play."
There was a lull in the conversation, and then…
Missy: "Bear, is this my fault?"
Bear: "No, it isn't."
Missy: "But if I wouldn't have gone into that building…"
Bear: "You were just in the wrong place at the wrong time. None of this is your fault."
Just then Missy got up and went over to where Bear was sitting. She sat down next to him and put her head on his chest. Bear wasn't expecting this, but he put his arm around her and looked over at Jennifer, who was across the room, watching. Whatever she might have been feeling didn't show.
Missy: "Did you used to know my mom?"
Bear paused a moment and looked over at Jennifer: "We were friends a long time ago - before you were around."
Missy: "How come you're not friends anymore?"
Jennifer didn't like where this was going, so she stepped in, "Honey, you better try to get some sleep."
Bear found a blanket in the Hummer and made a place for Missy to sleep. As Jennifer tucked her in,
Bear did some exploring in the barn. Towards the back he found an old motorcycle. Just then Jennifer walked up, crossed her arms, and said, "Of course there would be a motorcycle here."
Bear was tired and didn't want any drama.
As much as Jennifer wanted to avoid it, those old memories wouldn't stay in the past. They picked a heck of a time to surface. "I never got to hold my baby – our

baby." That did it. The dam had been breached. There was no stopping it now. "How was I supposed to get through it? We never talked about it." Bear had nothing to say in his own defense. How do you defend the indefensible? She continued, "You just shut down – like you're doing now. You didn't give me anything to work with. I gave it a couple months after the accident." Angrily, she went on, "You never pushed back." She waited for him to say something. Anything. Fuming, she turned around and walked away, then spun around to finish it. She erupted, "I've hated you for so long!" Then she pounded Bear on the chest over and over, crying and wailing, releasing a deep pain that she had carried inside for so long. She finally collapsed to the ground. After a minute she collected herself and said, "How could one person make so many bad choices?" Bear finally spoke up, "Look, I'm trying to -" Jennifer interrupted him, "I'm talking about myself, Bear!" This caught him by surprise. She continued, "I've spent the last ten years blaming you for everything." To which Bear replied, "There's plenty of blame to go around." She had to purge her soul, so she went on, "Yeah, you messed up, but I did too. I've never been willing to take a hard look at myself. We could die because of the choices I made. I wanted the good life – I took the easy way. I wasn't thinking about what was best for Missy." She paused, not knowing if she should admit what she thought might be her worst transgression. "Bear, I knew what Reece was. Deep down I knew." Bear's instinctive response was to comfort her, "You can't change what happened." Jennifer asked, "But how can I live with that?" Bear replied, "You don't think I've asked myself the same question?" She wanted to know more: "How did you deal with it?" He shrugged and said, "Not real well. Like you said, I shut down. We all have our coping mechanisms." Jennifer finally asked, "And where was God through all this?" Bear thought for a moment, not wanting to give her a pat answer, "I think he was trying to get my attention. He won't force anyone to get healed. I think he has a plan, though." "Assuming we don't die tonight," Jennifer added, crying and laughing at the same time. With a weak smile, Bear said, "You're just a barrel of sunshine." She came back around to their dire situation again, "I'm serious; we could all die." Bear commented, "I'm not too worried about death. I'm not crazy about pain, though." Jennifer could see he was trying to make the best of a bad situation, and also that he had lost everything for being willing to save her and Missy. She said, "Why do we only turn to God when we're out of options?" After thinking for a moment, Bear said, "If we had any idea how dangerous free will is, we'd give it back." Jennifer looked up at Bear, wanting to make a fresh start: "Bear... those awful things I said today..." Bear immediately shot back, "Forget about it." But she wouldn't have it: "That's what I've *always* done – just forgotten about it. I've never taken responsibility for the things I've said." Bear replied, "I probably deserved some of it." But Jennifer wouldn't let herself off the hook: "And what do you think I deserved? I thought I was better than you." She stood up and walked over to the wall. With tears streaming down her cheeks, she said, "I don't know if God even wants me anymore." Bear walked over to her and put his hands on her shoulders. He looked into her eyes and said, "I'll tell you what – if he'll take someone like me, he'll take you."

His words went deep inside her and seemed to unlock part of her soul. She gazed up at him, as if the last ten years had never happened. Bear felt it, too. He would have to be comatose not to feel ten years of passion wanting to be unleashed. Jennifer waited, half expecting him to kiss her, but he gently pushed her away instead, saying, "We really need to get some sleep."

After Jennifer had drifted off to sleep next to Missy, Bear was still awake. He looked at Jennifer, and whispered to himself, "Why are you so important?" As if answering Bear's question, Zavan burst onto the scene with blinding brilliance and grabbed Bear and Jennifer, one in each arm, and shot skyward. He went up and up, and then through a multi-colored tunnel. When they landed, they were in the balcony of a theater. They were looking out over a crowd of well-dressed people, apparently waiting for a concert to start. Bear and Jennifer were too stunned to say anything. They just looked around incredulously. Jennifer finally found her voice, and said to Zavan, "W-who...?" Zavan said, "Just watch." They went down the stairs and walked among the concert-goers. They must have been invisible, because no one noticed the two people walking with an angel. In the hall they found themselves within earshot of a scowling redhead who was talking on her cellphone: "I don't even know why I came tonight. I hate him. I'm filing papers tomorrow."

The concert was about to begin, so they went into the auditorium. A woman in her early twenties walked out onto the stage. She carried herself with an amazing air of grace and dignity. There was something familiar about her. It didn't take Jennifer long, as her mouth dropped open, "Missy," she whispered. Zavan smiled and grabbed them both and jumped straight up, through the ceiling and up into the night sky. As Missy began playing her violin, the sky churned. It began to spin clockwise until a passage opened up. A golden, glowing mist started to flow down through the portal and onto the auditorium. Bear felt his skin begin to tingle. Zavan brought them back to the balcony, where they witnessed something that was so far beyond their imagining, they couldn't believe what they were seeing. As Missy played, the golden mist permeated the building. They saw a shimmering being approach an older gentleman who was in obvious pain, and with just a touch the man's eyes shot open, and he looked around. A smile crept over his face as it was clear that the pain was gone. Their attention was drawn to a woman with gnarled, arthritic hands. They watched in awe as the mist swirled around her hands, and her fingers straightened out. She flexed and clenched her hands over and over. She was healed!

Zavan pointed out a middle-aged man and explained, "He has a long history of mental illness. Years of therapy and medication have had no effect." The shimmering figure approached him, reached into his head and pulled out a writhing spirit-snake, leaving his mind whole. When he sensed the change, he dropped to his knees and sobbed with joy. He knew his long nightmare was over.

The Recipient

On the other side of the auditorium they saw the same redhead who planned to divorce her husband. She was leaning up against him, crying, and said to him, "I'm so sorry – you didn't deserve any of this. Things are going to be different from now on."

Jennifer was unable to take it all in. Without turning away from the spectacle, she said, "This is about her; it's always been about her." Bear couldn't help but agree, "She's the recipient of an amazing gift. No wonder he's so desperate to get rid of her." The next thing Bear remembered is being back in the barn, and seeing Jennifer and Missy sleeping. He wasn't far behind them.

Dagon burst into the barn in full celestial mode as the three were sleeping. He waved his hand, and Bear and Jennifer were paralyzed. They could only watch as Dagon walked toward Missy. Zavan suddenly materialized between the two, with a fierce look on his face. For his own reason, he was visible only to Dagon. Jennifer and Bear couldn't understand why he stopped.
Zavan: "You overplayed your hand."
Dagon: "I play to win. You should know that."
Zavan: "There are rules."
Dagon: "Which I know just as well as you."
Zavan: "If you attack one of ours unjustly, there's a price to be paid."
Dagon: "Just couldn't help yourself, could you?"
Zavan: "Consider yourself warned."
Dagon disappeared into a puff of smoke. Jennifer, Bear and Missy only saw Dagon talking to the air in a language they didn't understand. All they knew is that

'it' was gone, and they could move again. Jennifer was the first to speak, "Bear, what the hell?" Bear replied, "Exactly. Let's get out of here."

The Recipient

The Recipient

Chapter seventeen

Possessed

The three were driving down a gravel road after they left the barn. So much had transpired in the last day. Each one was busy trying to make sense of everything. Missy had her headphones on and was glued to her tablet.

Jennifer: "What is it with you and dreams? You remember the dream from last night, don't you?"

Bear: I'm not sure that was a dream."

Jennifer: "What was it then?

Bear: "I don't know. Maybe we were in the future."

Bear glanced back at Missy. "The main thing is – you got a very special little girl there. You don't have to be a prophet to see that she's got a gift."

Jennifer: "And where do you fit in?"

Bear: "I'm going to keep her alive."

Jennifer gasped as she remembered the article she had copied from the library. She had forgotten about it during the chaos. "I almost forgot – I found this as I was doing some research at the library. It's from newspaper dated 1901." Bear's eyebrows shot up as he glanced at the headlines, which read, 'Disappearance of young violinist still a mystery'. He looked at Jennifer, who scanned the article and said, "Here... 'nine year old Shannon McQuade, an accomplished violinist, along with her mother, Olive McQuade, disappeared...'" Bear interjected, "Olive McQuade? That's my great-grandmother! You found that at the library?" Bear pulled to the side of the road to focus on what he was hearing.

Jennifer continued, "Let's see… details are sketchy… possibly an accidental drowning…" Bear frowned and said, "That doesn't sound right." Jennifer responded, "I guess fake news has been around for awhile." She paused as Bear was processing everything." She continued, "I made a copy of this when I saw the headline of the nine-year old violinist. What are the odds?" Bear responded in a quiet voice as he stared out the windshield, "It's no coincidence." Jennifer kept probing for more information. "You never talked about your family." Bear turned his head to look at her. "My family has a no-talk rule. Some things are off limits. This is one of them. From what I was able to find out, Olive kept a journal. They say she went crazy. There's even a rumor that she killed her daughter and herself. It's like a cloud that's been hanging over my family." Jennifer asked, "Do you know where that journal is? It might give us some answers." Bear took a deep breath and said, "It disappeared a long time ago." Then he added, "There is a possibility, though."

Bear drove onto a gravel road, which led to a cowpath, which led to the back side of his ranch. He knew better than to use the driveway. They were probably staking out the place. He parked out of sight of the main buildings, and they silently made their way into the barn. He went to the room where all the 'family history' stuff was stored. He usually referred to it as junk. He would eventually get around to sorting it out. After digging through piles of boxes, he finally found an antique trunk that looked like it hadn't been touched in decades. Strangely enough, it wasn't locked. As he opened the lid, three sets of eyes anxiously searched the inside of the trunk. Bear reached in and pulled out old photo albums, keepsakes, books, and files. He stacked them next to the trunk until it was empty. He went through the pile again, still not finding what he was looking for. He whispered, "I thought it would be in here." He glanced at the inside of the trunk, then the outside, then the inside again, with a puzzled look on his face. He reached into the bottom of the trunk and knocked on the bottom a few times in different spots. He took out a small pocket knife and pried up the edge of the bottom, and it began to come up. "False floor." He said, as he continued to pry it up. Jennifer reached in and pulled out a picture of a young woman. On the back some words were barely visible: 'Olive McQuade – ca. 1901'. She also pulled out a brown, leather bound book. Jennifer's eyes lit up, "The journal!" Missy put her finger to her lips and whispered, "Mom!" Jennifer handed the journal to Bear, who opened it and began scanning it. It was almost too much for Jennifer. She wanted answers. Details. Bear looked up and said, "She was having vivid nightmares." He turned it around for them to see – it was a drawing of... "That's him." Missy said, with a look of shock on her face. "He was after her too. Does it say what happened to them?" Bear responded, "Her writing ends here, but it continues with what looks like a man's handwriting. 'The spiritual battle has been getting more intense. I'm worried about them. We may be in over our heads...'

The Recipient

August 1901

*Olive threw the bedroom door open and shook Shannon's shoulder. "Get up, Shannon! We have to go **now**!" As groggy as she was, she noticed the urgency in her mother's voice. She knew something was very wrong. Mac was out of town on business, a fact which Dagon exploited. Olive had just awakened from an urgent dream that alerted her to the danger headed her way. In a flash they were on horseback riding into the darkness.*

Not too far away, Dagon watched as four men, his human protégés, mounted their horses. The leader said, "It's time to finish this." They raced off into the woods with two huge, ferocious dogs following. The trail eventually split off, one part heading south. The decided to split up to cover more ground.

The ground was flying by underneath them as Shannon held onto her mother for dear life. Their horse was getting tired, though. He couldn't keep up that pace all night. Olive stopped to let him rest for a minute. In the silence, she heard horses behind her galloping hard. She could either keep running or try to hide. She knew her horse was about done, so she led them into the undergrowth. Minutes later the two men stopped to listen a stone's throw away from Olive. She held her breath. Something must be guiding them. The dog sniffed and growled. One of the men gave the dog a command, and it bounded toward Olive's hiding place. There was no place left to hide.

The Recipient

Three days later, Mac had gotten the sheriff's message, and the two men were talking in a dark hallway. The sheriff opened the door, allowing Mac to see two figures on tables, each covered with a blanket. As Mac fought back tears, the sheriff broke the silence. "The horse led us to them."   Mac slowly approached the tables, then the sheriff put his hand on Mac's arm and said, "Mac, you don't want to see them like this. Remember them the way they were."

Unseen by either men, Dagon was in the room, feeding off Mac's pain. 'There will be no portal in this generation," he whispered to himself.

Jennifer, Bear and Missy were sitting in stunned silence by the trunk. The realization of the gravity of their situation was hitting Jennifer. Staring straight ahead, she said, barely audibly, "We're gonna die." Missy's eyes were closed and her lips were moving, like she was praying silently. Bear grabbed Jennifer's face and made her look at him. She repeated, "They're going to kill us." Bear said to her, "I'm not going to let that happen." Unconvinced, she said back, "What can you do? Do you know what we're up against?" Bear shot back, "All I know is, I'm supposed to be here. And I'm not going to let that happen." He enunciated each word for emphasis. That helped her calm down. "I'll be right back," said Bear, as he went to see if there were any cars patrolling the road.

The Recipient

Jennifer looked at Missy and said, "I've got to get you to safety. You shouldn't be involved in this." Missy took a deep breath and said, "Mom, I'm already involved. You told me I have a destiny, remember? Did you mean that, or was that just stuff grownups say to kids?" Jennifer was caught off guard. Missy was sounding more like an adult than a child. All Jennifer could think of to say was, "Sweetie, we're in real danger." With a display of wisdom and clear thinking that she had never heard before, Missy said, "I know, Mom. I've been thinking about this a lot. You think I'm too young to understand, but I know more than you think I do. I know about the war we're in, and about the portal." Missy paused to let her mom process what she just said. She continued, knowing full well that she was about to drop the bomb. "Sometimes in wars"- Jennifer cut her off, "Don't! I'm not"- Missy reached over and grabbed her hand, and continued, "Mom, however many years I get, I want to make them count. I'm here for a reason. I've made my choice. I need you to be okay with that." Bear walked back over and whispered, "I hope I'm not interrupting, but we have to go."

Soon they were back in the Hummer, speeding down the road.

Jennifer: "There's got to be a way we can take our lives back. "

Bear: "What could we use for leverage against Reece?"

Jennifer: "That's a tough one. I don't know enough about his business. Or his secrets."

Bear: "What if we had evidence that he was the one who killed us?"
Jennifer: "But we don't – he didn't."
Bear: "You're not thinking like a criminal. He has a collection of expensive swords and daggers, right?"
Jennifer: "Right, and all of them are insured and registered in his name."
Bear: "If one of those were found with the blood of the murder victims on it…"
Jennifer: "He'd go to jail, but that wouldn't stop him from putting a contract out on us."
Bear: "What if he knew the knife was out there? We could hold it over his head. He wouldn't dare take any action against you."
Jennifer: "So you want to break into the house and steal a knife."
Bear: "It's our only chance to even the score."
Jennifer: "Okay, but I'm going with."
Bear: "It's too risky."
Jennifer: "But I know the code, and where the security cameras are."
Bear: "You'll just have to walk me through it."
Jennifer: "The security camera in back isn't working. You can get there using the trail in back, but you'll have to use an ATV or motorcycle."
Bear: "Maybe Neal can help us with that."

Soon they arrived at Neal's house. Bear explained the situation, and Neal was happy to let him take the cycle. Jennifer gave him the security system code and a worried look, and Bear was off. When he arrived at Bernell's house, he parked the cycle on the trail, out of sight, and when he was sure Reece wasn't home, he went to the back door and entered the code. After he got in the house, he wasted no time going to the den.

Meanwhile, Reece was in his car when his phone made a warning sound. He looked at it and made a quick U-turn and drove toward home.

Bear quickly found the dagger that Reece seemed so proud of. How poetic that it would be his downfall. Bear's heart started pounding when he heard a car coming in the driveway. He didn't think Reece would be that close to home. *Was that a coincidence? No point in figuring that out now. Run!* He heard the front door open, then slam shut. He knew he didn't have time to get to the exit. Where to hide? He went to the room he had been working on and stopped there to listen. He heard Reece walking around, then getting closer. He hid behind the door... it opened. He was inches away from Reece, with only a door between them. Bear held his breath. The door finally closed. Reece left, and Bear was able to make it out.

Bear hopped back on the cycle and went to the scene of the 'murder', where he covered the knife in blood. He took pictures of it and put it in a plastic bag. He slipped the knife into a cubbyhole in the abandoned building, then texted the location and picture to Jennifer. He didn't want to have the 'just in case this doesn't work' talk. His next move had to be audacious. This wasn't the time for caution. At least that's how he was feeling. There was only one thing left to do: confront Reece. He rode straight there, then thought about the onsite security cameras. He pulled his hood up over his head and kept his shades on. He would try to avoid facing the cameras directly. That would have to do. He walked right in the front door, and into Reece's office.

Bear: "This ends now."

Reece: "This is unexpected. Saves me the trouble of finding you."

Bear: "Jennifer's dead."

Reece: "Really?"

Bear: "Yeah. You killed her – with this." He pulled out his phone and showed him the picture of the knife. "Do you recognize it? It's covered with her blood and your fingerprints."

Reece: "You're new at this, aren't you? Now let me guess the rest. I agree to go away and never come back, and that knife stays securely tucked away in some obscure safe deposit box. If one of you were to have an unfortunate accident, that knife would end up on the desk of the police commissioner the next day."

Bear: "That's about right. I'd call that a draw."

Reece: "A draw… You know what they say – a tie is like kissing your sister. And by the way, I own the police commissioner. I prefer to win, and as I told you earlier, sometimes you have to break the rules to do that."

Right after that, the door to the office opened, and Jennifer and Missy walked in accompanied by two other men Bear hadn't seen before. Missy was clutching her little violin case like a security blanket. His heart sank into his stomach; he felt sick and hopeless. And angry. The smug look on Reece's face. The arrogance. *This isn't over yet. His pride will trip him up. He'll make a mistake.* But Reece continued, "A nice bluff, I must say. A little red number five mixed with corn syrup, throw in a dead man's switch – I'll give you an A for effort. But next time… oh wait – there won't be a next time. By the way, I figured out where we met in the past. I knew I had seen you before. You were that poor slob I ran into with my car all those years ago. It's a good thing I was drunk – I walked away without a scratch. Ironic, isn't it, when you're drunk, your body is more relaxed – less likely to suffer injuries. I didn't figure it out until after we had our sparring match. You used wrestling moves. I remembered that the guy I hit was a wrestler, so I did a little digging. You were never all that great. No fire, I guess." He motioned to his goons to take them to the back of the warehouse. Reece followed them and said, "Make yourselves comfortable," then went to the far side of the warehouse to talk to his men. Reece asked them, "What about the other guy? The one whose house they were at?" The one who looked like an ex pro football player said, "Don't worry – he won't be bothering us. I knocked him out cold and tied him up." The other man chimed in, now a little worried, "Uh, your tech guy said he lived alone. He doesn't know where we are." Reece's eyes narrowed. "If you recall, my instructions were, no loose ends. My finder did his part; you were supposed to do yours. Do you know what no loose ends means?" They were both silent. Reece continued, "It means this." He pulled out his pistol and shot them both point blank. They fell to the floor, dead before they even hit the ground. Now the odds were a little more even. Bear, Jennifer and Missy were frozen with horror. Without stopping even for a moment to acknowledge the lives that had just been cut short, Reece walked over and lifted his gun up to Bear's forehead. Bear knew it was now or never. All or nothing. In a split second, he understood that everything he had ever experienced was preparation for this moment. After making a conscious decision to overrule the fear that was paralyzing him, he hit Reece's wrist and forearm in a way that sent the gun flying across the room and down into a floor grate. Bear swung at Reece and connected with the side of his head. Reece had been training far too long to be taken out by a surprise move. He came back with a straight shot to Bear's head, followed by a knee in the gut, sending him sprawling to the floor. Jennifer was holding onto Missy for dear life. While Bear sprang back up, Reece said, "I had hoped we could do this the easy way." Reece came at Bear with a volley of punches, most of which he avoided or deflected. The one that caught him sent him the floor, bleeding. Reece didn't seem to be in a hurry to finish him off. He almost seemed to be enjoying this. Bear wouldn't stay down, so Reece came at him again, using well-rehearsed martial arts moves. Bear was desperately ducking and weaving, knowing he was outmatched, but watching for an opening. Reece sounded off again, "I'm afraid there's no tapping out in this match," and aimed a kick at Bear's solar plexus, but Bear was able to sidestep and trap the leg between his left arm and his side and used his momentum to swing Reece around right into the sheetrock wall. It wasn't enough to stop him, though. He caught Bear with a right cross, and he went down again, next to a bucket of sand. He moved a little slower getting up, but as he did, he grabbed a handful of sand, and whispered just loud enough for Reece to hear him, "Sometimes you gotta break the rules." He threw the sand in Reece's face, causing him to turn his head just long enough for Bear to tackle him. As they were struggling for position, Bear yelled to Jennifer, "Get the gun!" Now the fight was on the ground – Bear's advantage. The next few moments were instinct and muscle memory from many years of grappling, as Jennifer was trying unsuccessfully to get the grate open. Bear got Reece's left arm behind his back and wrenched it upward toward his head, resulting in a loud crack, and a scream. Finally Bear took Reece's head and slammed in onto the floor, leaving him unconscious. As Bear was breathing heavily, he said to Reece, "Do you see any fire now?"

Bear walked over to Jennifer and Missy and put his arms around them and said, "It's over." They turned to go to the front of the warehouse and put this whole ordeal behind them. Just then they heard a sound coming from Reece's direction. They turned around just in time to see Dagon turn into smoke and swirl around Reece, who was still laying on the floor. He entered Reece through his nose and mouth, which caused his body to spasm violently. His eyes opened, now all black. He got up and twisted his left arm until the shoulder popped back into place. Then he spoke in a guttural voice, "It's not over til I win." Jennifer was at an eleven on her one-to-ten scale of what she could handle. She shouted, "Reece!" at the top of her voice. Dagon answered, "Save your breath – he can't hear you." As he moved toward them, Bear confronted Reece, now possessed by Dagon, and breathed out a prayer, "I told you I'd protect them, but I need your help." Zavan whispered back a response, "It's on the way." Bear looked around as if he had heard something. Back to the matter at hand. He approached Reece and put everything he had into a right hook, that connected to Reece's face. He shook it off like it was a mosquito bite. He lunged at Reece but was flung away with one swipe. Reece said, "Is that all you got?" He took a deep, exaggerated breath, like he was smelling something, and continued to taunt Bear, "Power is intoxicating. It's better than any drug." Bear felt all but helpless as Reece threw him across a worktable, then up against a wall. He kept getting back up, staying between Reece and Jennifer. Reece said, "You don't seem to know when you're beat." Zavan said to himself, "He's too strong. We need backup." Reece went over to Bear and grabbed him by the neck, jerked him to his feet, and marched him forward. He announced, "Looks like you failed. Again. No one can stop me now." Still invisible, Zavan moved closer to Bear and whispered these words into his ear: "If you want this to work, you have to commit to it." Bear had heard those words before. He had spoken them to Ty. Message received and understood. Zavan stood back and yelled, "NOW!" Bear heard it, and reached back with his left arm, clamped onto Reece's right arm, arched into him, and took Reece down in a modified over and under throw. Landing on the ground, Bear followed up instinctively and wrapped him up in a choke hold. Dagon's possession of Reece had given him supernatural strength, but now he had no leverage, and was unable to breathe. He grabbed Bear's arm and squeezed. It felt like his forearm would snap in two. Zavan immediately went to Missy and whispered something in her ear. She gave a puzzled look but got out her violin and began to play. Bear was still in a life and death struggle with Reece (or Dagon), who had begun to levitate a few inches off the floor. As Missy became more focused, the music got louder, and Bear's chest began to burn. It was right where Zavan had inserted the stones of fire. He could actually feel the three of them burning, glowing. Dagon could feel it, too, and was screaming like a banshee, trying to get away from it, but Bear held on for dear life. Now it was Zavan's turn. He reached inside Reece and got a hold of Dagon by the neck and began to pull. He knew this was his last stand, and did *not* want to come out. Missy realized she was affecting the outcome, so she got a little closer, and played with even greater intensity. Dagon began to vibrate, and Zavan pulled harder. One final heave, and Dagon was completely out of Reece's body, which went limp. Bear scrambled over to Missy and Jennifer, sensing this was not over. Dagon stood to his feet, and Zavan materialized in full celestial mode. His face briefly turned into the face of a lion and he let out a roar that shook the building. Bear, Jennifer and Missy looked at the spectacle in front of them without moving a muscle, hardly believing it was real.

Zavan reached over his shoulder and grabbed a sword that had been invisible up until that point. Dagon did the same, and said, "I've been waiting for this for a long time." Zavan slashed first, only to be blocked by Dagon, who came back swinging ferociously. Every time the swords clashed, it resonated through the metal framework of the building. Dagon thought his rage was an advantage, but in reality, it was causing him to lose control. They both paused for a moment, then swung at each other at the same time. Their swords connected with such force that both blades shattered. Zavan wasted no time lamenting over his sword and lunged at Dagon with a kick that sent him hurtling into a wall.

The Recipient

Dagon came back with a vengeance, throwing a flurry of punches, sending Zavan to the ground. He rolled through and got back up and rushed at Dagon, knocking him into a metal pillar, bending it slightly. The next few seconds were a burst of vicious activity that the human eye could barely follow. Finally, Zavan landed a blow that knocked Dagon to the ground, momentarily stunned. allowing Zavan to meet eyes with Missy, who had stopped playing. Zavan mouthed the word 'play' to her. She understood and began playing her violin again. Zavan looked at Dagon, who was still on the ground, unable to get up, then back at Missy. She hit a note that seemed to make Dagon wince in pain, then held it. Zavan joined in, singing in the same pitch. Dagon was writhing on the floor, then disappeared in a puff of smoke. Zavan let out a huge sigh of relief, then looked back at Missy and mouthed the words, 'thank you', then disappeared in a flash of light.

Bear collapsed to the ground, exhausted. For about a minute, nobody said a word. Finally, Missy asked, "Are they gone?" Bear said, "I think so." When they made their way to the front of the warehouse, Bear looked up and saw Neal holding a 9mm Glock pointed in his direction and froze. A thousand thoughts went through Bear's mind. *Neal is one of them. Why didn't I see this coming?* Neal fired the gun, but Bear wasn't hit. They turned around in time to see Reece fall to the floor, holding the gun he had rescued from under the grate. Of all the questions he had, he just asked, "How did you find us?" Neal shook his head, and they said together, "You don't want to know."

Before long, police cars and ambulances were all over the place. Neal was long gone, because he didn't need that kind of attention. He had worked out a story for them to tell the police that sounded plausible and kept him out of it. It was clear that Neal had done this type of thing before. They wouldn't have been able to pull this off without him.

Bear was sitting in an ambulance, listening to a detective who was trying to get more information out of him: "Can you go over the timeline again for me?" Bear sighed; he looked as tired and beat up as he was. Bear saw Jennifer and Missy sitting in the back of a police cruiser, looking like they just wanted to go home. But where was home for them now? Jennifer and Bear locked eyes, and all the sound seemed to fade away for a moment. It was as if they were the only two people in the world.

The Recipient

Chapter eighteen

United

Bear pulled into the hospital parking lot. He found out that Rob came through alive, but not necessarily unscathed. No big surprise; Mossad training is not for the faint of heart. The explosion took out two of Reece's men and did a lot of damage to the house, but Rob came out of it with a through and through gunshot wound. Bear figured he should pay him a visit, because if it wasn't for him, who knows how things might have turned out. He also noticed that there seemed to be a certain chemistry between the two – like they had been friends for a long time even though they just met. Maybe it was the camaraderie that soldiers experience in battle.

Bear found the room Rob was in, and walked in carrying a red balloon that said, 'get well soon'.

Bear: "These nurses are tough! I had to convince them that I was your brother so they'd let me in!"

Rob: "Did they see the resemblance?" Rob laughed, then winced in pain. "Ow, I can't laugh. It hurts when I laugh." He also sensed the kinship between the two. Instant friendship. "You know, I don't think we've been properly introduced."

Bear: "That's true. Holding me at gunpoint doesn't make a good first impression."

Rob: "I'm Rob Drescher, and you already know I'm with Mossad."

Bear: "And I'm Bear McQuade. Handyman."

Rob: "Handyman, huh? And I'm the one that got shot."
Bear: "The irony! I thought they teach you to dodge bullets!" Bear pulled up a chair and sat down. "So now that your cover is blown, what's next?"
Rob: "My time with Mossad is almost up. You know, I kind of like it here. I might just stick around and start a fugitive retrieval service. I could use somebody who can handle a shotgun, and who I can trust."
Bear: "Bear the bounty hunter!" He laughed at the idea. "I don't think I can handle any more adrenaline right now. I better stick to what I know."

After they had talked for a while, Bear got up to leave. "I better let you rest." He got to the door and turned around and said, "Fugitive retrieval, huh? Well, you never know."

"Come on in" Jennifer said to Bear. He had gone to the mansion as they were packing up some of their things. She didn't want to spend any more time there than necessary – she wanted to close that chapter of her life. It didn't feel like home anymore. To tell the truth, it never really did feel like home. Jennifer had begun the hard work of confronting herself. No more taking the easy way. It was hard, but it felt good. No more Jennifer the trophy wife - she wanted more from herself than that. She knew she had been given another chance, and she was not going back to her old patterns. Call it a rebirth. If love came into her life again, this time it would be based on something real. She knew where it had to start, so she said to him, "Bear, what you did for me, for us, was so far above and beyond…" Bear held up his hand to stop her, and said, "I appreciate the gratitude, and it looks good on you, by the way, but it's not necessary. I think you two did more for me than I did for you." Jennifer knew he had never been comfortable being on the receiving end of effusive thank-you's, but she needed to say it. She had also noticed a big change in Bear. She told him, "You do look different – even from a few days ago." Bear replied, "I guess it took all that to get it through my head that I'm here for a reason."

A little later as they were sitting at the bar in the kitchen over coffee, Bear noticed Missy putting her favorite doll in her suitcase. When she saw Bear, she ran over to see him. Bear reached into his pocket and said to her, "You know what I found out?" She responded, "What?" Bear pulled out the star she had made for him and said, "This really worked! I don't know what I would have done without it!"

After Missy had gone into the other room, Bear said to Jennifer, "She's had a rough few days - I hope she can sleep it off." Jennifer replied, "We need to go someplace for a while where absolutely nothing happens. I'll gladly take a few weeks of boredom." Bear glanced at Missy and said, "Kids are pretty resilient. She'll be okay; she has a great mom." Jennifer took a sip of coffee, then shook her head. *Bear is a smart guy. Why hasn't he been able to figure this out? I thought the moment he saw her he would put two and two together. The instant Missy saw him, there was a connection. Can't he see how she lights up whenever he's around?*

The Recipient

Didn't he ever look at the timeline? Ten years? Unable to hold back a smile, she said, "Bear, you're such an idiot." He opened his mouth to say something, but nothing came out. An idea was forming in his mind that he had never even considered. This was his deer in the headlights moment. The dream. The connection they shared. Duh. Bear looked over at Missy, then back at Jennifer, who was giving him that, 'you can't possibly be that dense' look. Bear's mind went into overdrive: joy, grief, confusion, anger. Why had the best thing in his life been withheld from him for so long? How could she do that to him? Without a word, Bear stood up and walked to the front door and left, without even turning around for one last look.

Jennifer was left with her thoughts. *I never told him about Missy. I was so hurt and angry because of what happened. He didn't deserve that happiness. It was my way of punishing him. I was so consumed by bitterness I didn't see that I was punishing Missy too. God gave me another chance, but is it too late now?*

Zavan was in his office, writing in his journal:
Why do I still question the wisdom of the creator? I was following the directive I had been given – to prevent Bear from realizing that he was Missy's father. I withheld that knowledge from him because it was necessary for him to go through the entire process, painful as it was, on his own. Otherwise it would have turned into either an obsession or a burden and clouded his judgment. As counterintuitive as it may seem, this was the best path to his restoration.

The Recipient

Bear figured it was time to send Ty an email:

Hey Ty,

Remember that dream you told me about? The one with me in the coffin? I figured out what it means. It wasn't about my premature death – it meant that parts of my past needed to die. That's why I was in the eighties' garb! And I think (I hope) that whatever needed to die, is now stone cold dead!

Keep dreaming!
Bear

Six months later

It was a beautiful day for a drive on a country road - there was not a cloud in the sky. There was a wine red 1970 convertible coupe sitting by the side of the road, whose occupants had just changed seats. Neal was now driving, and Bear was the passenger for its maiden 'voyage'. Neal fiddled with the radio dial until Sweet Home Alabama was blasting out the high-performance speakers. They both put on their sunglasses, buckled up, and Neal punched it, sending gravel flying behind them. The car ran like a dream as the scenery flew by them. All the work Bear put into it had paid off. The naysayers were wrong - it wasn't too far gone to be restored. It just took a lot of work, a lot of patience, and a lot of love.

____

The Recipient

The stench of sulfur was more intense than ever in Dagon's subterranean lair, where he was nursing his wounds even as he was making plans for his comeback. With an increasingly unhinged look in his eyes, he muttered to himself, "Zavan… McQuade… next time… take no prisoners…" He was frantically walking up and down the rows of bookshelves, searching for an idea, a weakness, anything he could use to take revenge and reclaim his status. "Next time…"

Bear had gotten past the whole ugly ordeal of losing Dusty. It had been a long process – it's hard enough to lose a horse, but for him to have been killed out of sheer spite took it to another level. Dusty had been buried in the middle of the pasture, marked with a pile of rocks. Bear was tempted to leave it without any markers, to be able to forget about that part of his life. The old Bear might have been okay with that, but he had a new outlook now. The past is just that – past. The memories no longer brought pain with them.

Bear was brushing his new gelding, Duke. Duke was a beautiful Morgan with a black mane and tail, and white socks on all four legs just above the hooves, and a white star on his forehead. Like Dusty, Duke loved going on the trails. Bear heard footsteps coming from behind him. He turned around, and it was Jennifer, wearing her new snakeskin cowboy boots, form-fitting blue jeans, and a mischievous look in her eyes. Bear grabbed her and picked her up and pushed her against Duke. He looked into her eyes, then kissed her. She wrapped her arms around his neck and kissed him back. It felt so natural, that is, until Missy rode up on her horse and covered her eyes and said, "Ewww!" She couldn't hold back a smile, though. She finally had a relationship with the father she had never known. She didn't mind sharing him with her mom.

Before long the three of them were racing across the clearing on their horses at a full gallop. Jennifer was on her buckskin quarter horse, and Missy was keeping up with them on her appaloosa. No Shetland pony for her - she was able to handle a full-size horse! As the wind whipped at his face, Bear thought back to the time not too long ago when he had worked through the anger he had toward Jennifer for not telling him about Missy. All that time lost. Wasted. But was it really? Logically, it was an easy decision – let it go, and the family can be united. Everyone wins. But bitterness is not logical; it's like darkness, like a poison that seeps into your bloodstream. He could feel it encroaching, and he recognized where it would take him. He had experienced light, and he wanted no part of darkness any more. He no longer feared the unknown, the mystical. He could embrace the visions and dreams, because now he trusted the source. For the first time in a long time, things finally made sense.

A lone figure was watching them from the edge of the forest. Zavan felt such a sense of pleasure at seeing his work come to fruition. There is no greater thrill for a celestial being, or a human for that matter, than seeing the creator's perfect plan worked out. Kiandra suddenly appeared next to him. "You were right – he came through." Zavan replied to her, "Do you think he knows this is just the beginning?" Kiandra answered the question with her own, "The question is, do you think he's ready to face the illuminati?" Zavan smiled and said, "He will be."

The Recipient

Prologue

Bear was awakened by the song of a bright red cardinal sitting on a branch just outside his window, somehow reminding him that this was a new day. There was one thing he needed to do in order to put the final nail in the coffin of his past.

Bear pulled into the parking lot of a company that specialized in monuments. His order was finally ready to pick up. The attendant wheeled it over to his pickup, and they loaded it into the bed. His trip to the cemetery was not what he expected; that familiar sense of dread was nowhere to be found.

Bear arrived at the tiny gravesite and pulled up the aluminum marker that read 'Baby Boy McQuade'. He maneuvered the granite headstone into place that read 'Casey Brian', then sat down crossed-legged on the ground so he could sort out his thoughts. It wasn't like he was saying good-bye; it was more like he felt a sense of completion, like he had just put the final piece of a puzzle in place.

While he was sitting there, the scenery in his mind shifted. He was still in the cemetery, but he was also seeing that meadow that Zavan had shown him, that place that no words could describe. He didn't know how, but he was in two places at once. He heard several children chanting in a singsong way, "It's Casey's turn, it's Casey's turn," as he saw a line of children emerge from the forest. It looked like they were playing follow the leader, and it was Casey's turn to lead! Bear took a breath to call out to his son, but before he could say anything, he heard a voice from behind him, "He can't see you." It was Zavan. As the questions began to form in Bear's mind, Zavan spoke again, "It's best this way, for reasons that are beyond your understanding. Just trust the father." Bear knew he was right.

The scene in front of him began to fade, and voices of the children became more and more distant, until the whole thing was just a memory. He looked around – he was back at the cemetery. As he got up and walked back to his pickup, he realized that no matter what life threw at him, no matter what situations he would encounter, he was going to be okay.

As he got into his pickup and drove away, the thought came to him:

The two best days of your life are the day you were born, and the day you find out why.

THE END

(or is it?)